# MY BEST FRIEND'S DAD

Older Man and Younger Woman Romance, First-Time Sex, Taboo Short Stories, and more!

By

Roby Palm

# PAGE LEFT INTENTIONALLY BLANK

# TABLE OF CONTENTS

# MY BEST FRIEND'S DAD IS MY CRUSH

Before I washed my palms and grinned, I placed the last package in the back of my Jeep. He finally got it all ready for the next year. My first time away from home and I was both excited and nervous about this new adventure. I've never been too far away from Lincoln, Nebraska before. I knew it was going to be difficult, college in another town, but my best friend, Diana, was going to be with me. We met in the first grade, she had just moved to town with her mom from Los Angeles, California.

We've learned that we've both been single mom kids and we've been trapped together ever since. It is incredible how things could move really fast. I was specifically surprised because I consider myself an introvert who is always weary of going out. As a matter of fact, we're ready to go to UCLA together now! Diana was there, and she spent every summer there with her dad who lived in the area. Yeah, it was going to be a solo trip out there for me. We were going to stay with her brother, who said he had more than enough space for us to stay. Given the price of the dorms there, we were more than pleased to have free housing.

"Erin!" My mom came out of the house with a little cooler in her hand. I felt bad leaving her home, she'd never been lonely before. It's always been me and her, it's just her now. I made a promise to Diana's mom to take care of her and contact me if she wanted anything. I was nervous, but mom said she wasn't. She was going to a "run" without the children around us.

"Mom, I told you I was going to be fine and pick up food along the way," I told her as I closed the back of my jeep and took the cooler from her. I switched to the passenger side and opened the door, setting the cooler on the concrete.

"I don't let my kid spend her money on fast food all the way to California. What if you get stuck somewhere and need food?" she said, staring worriedly at her face as she followed me around the car. I had to promise that I would call her every few hours to keep her calm. She originally tried to get me to agree to call hourly, and I told her that it was too much. We have come to a compromise. Email daily and call every couple of hours.

"Thank you, Dad," I said as I looked inside the refrigerator to find my favorite soda, drinks, snacks, and a few sandwiches nestled inside with ice to keep it cold. It wasn't enough to last 36 hours to get there, but it was enough to cover me for a while.

"You're welcome. You'd better get going if you're going to make it there on time. Diana's mom said that Diana's dad is waiting for you before dark tomorrow. Don't drive exhausted, if you just need to sit and rest email all of us and we know that you're going to be there later than expected and that you're free. I want to know the minute you get there." She kept talking as I held her close and gave her a kiss on the ear. She kept me close as she finished speaking, "And enjoy the next few weeks before school begins. I hear that California is beautiful.""I'll, to all of it. I'll call you as we agreed and enjoy my time there. It's only a few months before the break. I'll be back for the holidays." I gave her a last squeeze before I turned to my Jeep and turned it on. I'm going to pull out of our path, wave a farewell, and press the go button on my GPS. California, I'm coming here!

Hours later———-I hope this is it, I said to myself as I pulled into a driveway blocked by a fence. I could see from outside the gate that this was a huge house. It was bigger than my home and backyard. Geez, was Diana's dad famous or something? I only met the man once, he was at Diana's sweet 16th birthday party, he seemed to be down to earth and calm... This is not necessarily what I would have predicted. Okay, you know what they're doing, don't judge the cover text. I believe his IT firm is doing more than Diana said. I picked up my cell phone and hit the phone to find my best friend's number, hit the send on finding it. I got out of the car with the phone in my ear, listening to the ring as I looked around for a button to get in or something. This is going to take a bit of getting used to if this is the place.

"Hi Erin, are you still here?" asked Diana's voice on the phone.

"Um, I'm not sure," I responded uncertainly, taking the phone out of my ear and turning the volume down. "I'm at the entrance, and the number on it fits the address you sent me.""Yeah, let me get there. Give me a minute." She hung up before I could respond.

Yeah, now I think I'm just going to wait. I stepped toward the gate and stared at it at the front yard. Nice dark green lawn, roses lined up on the outside of the building. It seemed like almost every room on the second floor had a balcony added to it, so you could have a view of the yard. The house itself was a light tan bricked structure, the wall that lined the outside of the property seemed to suit. The gate was like a thick wood, woven into a pattern that looked like a tree.

Suddenly, the front door of the house opened and my best friend emerged, and she started to run when she saw that it was really me. "You're here! You did it!" Diana opened the door and took me into an embrace as she jumped up and down. We split apart after a minute. I was staring at her. It's been two months since we graduated from high school, and she left. She also looked amazing at 5'5, "sun-kissed skin", long blond hair, hazel eyes, medium build and boobs and butt that matched her figure. She was, as some people told her, a knock-out. She never believed any of them and, like most women, saw faults in every part of her body. She was wearing exercise shorts and an oversized shirt. It was almost 9 p.m. in this time zone, so she was in the night it was. I asked, trying to relax in a comfortable place other than a Jeep and a hole in the wall motel, could I stay long enough to take a few hours of sleep before hitting the road again?

Diana's face turned into a shocked look when she remembered she hadn't welcomed me in and we were still standing outside the house." Ah, shit! Sure, sure! Dad's got a driveway on his side, just follow the drive and there's a garage. He opened up a spot for you. I will just gladly show you. She hopped up on the passenger side, pushing things out of the way and leaning between her legs since the foot was taken up. I climbed in and turned the jeep over before following her orders. "Is your dad here? Maybe we need any help moving things in? Any milk, too? I'm getting hungry!" I smiled at her as I stepped into the open section of the garage, four cars match." Dad's still at work. He wanted to be here when you came since he hadn't seen you for years, but he was calling from work. I might order a pizza. "Dominoes are still good for you?" she asked. We got out and walked into the house. She opened up her phone and found the Domino's app and started ordering our regular load of food. We loved to eat. Any time we're together, there's food between us. I'm not sure what I was expecting when I came in, maybe fancy and expensive stuff, but it all seemed easy. It had all your basic house.

Diana and I smiled and held each other as she led me around. She showed me her bedroom that was great for her with pinkish walls and a canopy bed with curtains. She had a small entertainment center with a TV set and a DVD player. There were two Love sac bags in front of her. There was a desk in the corner of the room, filled with school books and papers that she had already gathered for classes. Her wardrobe was another room on its own, filled with all she wanted. Diana took me through another curtain, leading to a bathroom with two sinks, a mirror, a vanity, and a spacious upstairs tub. If I had to imagine that you might fit a few people in it.

"The bathroom separates our rooms. And, if we need each other, we can just walk through here. But I had dad put locks on both doors for privacy. Are you able to see your room? Dad said if you want to change it, you should let him know. Oh, and choose a paint color. I said purple would fit, but he wanted to ask you first. Like I don't know my best friends favorite color"

My bedroom was just like hers with white walls. I had a canopy bed with white sheets and a blanket, but without a curtain around the edges, there was a small entertainment center with a flat-screen TV and a DVD player and a desk in the corner. Diana led me to my bedroom where I could have stayed. Everything I had was going to fit in. I think I'm going to love this while it's going to last. I hugged Diana and thanked her for having me to stay with her and her dad for the next four years. I was feeling very lucky, and maybe a little overwhelmed by the size of it all, but it would be nice.

After catching up with some more music in her room while we were inhaling pizza and cinnastics, we decided it was time to turn in. Diana and I were planning to move my things to my room in the morning, hoping that her dad would be at home to help, otherwise we'd have to hunt down a strong man as Diana said it with a smile. I walked to my new room, turned into an oversized shirt that Diana lent to me, and crawled under thick, warm blankets before falling asleep.

I woke up the next morning to my phone ringing loudly, I grabbed it before it dropped off the nightstand next to my pillow. I wiped my eyes as I was trying to make a name out on the phone. It started buzzing before I could give an answer. The computer shifted to tell me that I got 20 calls and 40 texts from "MOM." Well, shit, I was thinking about myself when I realized that I forgot to call my mom last night. Ugh, darn it, man. I prepared myself for her, either weeping or yelling on the phone. I looked at the time, and now it was 8 a.m., California time... that means it's 10 a.m. Yes, in Omaha. She's got to be worried sick by now. Sitting up and hit the mother's dial button and listened to the sound.

"Erin Richardson, you're in a lot of trouble!" my mom screamed at me on the phone. Wow, not a good morning or anything. I really must have been worried about her.

"I'm sorry, Mom. I've gotten here, and I'm totally distracted by calling you," I replied, hoping to calm her down a little.

"Sorry! I've been trying to call not only you but also Diana and her father. No one is listening. Is there anyone with you? Are you sure you're in the right place? Where are you?" she said in her voice worriedly, but I could still see her pacing in the middle of the living room, her arm waving in frustration.

"I'm at Diana's dad's house. I don't know why anyone is answering your phone calls, but mum, it's 8 o'clock in the morning. I know Diana doesn't get up that early because her dad worked all night so maybe he's sleeping?" I replied, I got up and walked through the bathroom to Diana's space. Hey, she's been laid out on her bunk. I took a pair of her workout shorts from her dresser and put them on. "I'm going downstairs and I'm trying to see if Mr. Anderson's car is here.

Diana is still asleep.""Alright, as long as you're safe, Megan, I'm just concerned. I haven't got to the party yet because I had to make sure you arrived safely," she laughed. I laughed as she began asking me about the location and what it was like. Unlike me, she just met Diana's dad once, but most definitely she learned plenty about him from Diana's mother. I said what I could, she, ohh'd and ah'd as I described the house.

I walked into the kitchen to see a shirtless man in a loose pajama chest, preparing what looked like pancakes. I stopped and stared at him as my mom thought about stuff going back home. Here and there, he had smooth skin and freckles on his arms, dark hair sprouting in random spots on his upper back. He has short dark brown hair that looks as if he has rolled out of bed and disturbed as if he got up in a strange way. I cleared my throat, not understanding who this guy was or how to get his attention, it seemed to be the best way to show my presence in the room. The man jumped and spun around, nearly knocking the pan off the burner. I took a breath and my eyebrows flew up in surprise. Holy hell, this guy was really good looking! He had a thin stubbly beard, with glasses wired over his dark brown eyes, short hairs crossed his chest and led down into his pajamas in a relaxed way. While not muscular, he was lean and very tall. If I had to presume he'd have to be about six feet tall. His eyes widened in surprise when he saw me, and then he smiled as if he knew who I was.

"Erin?" he asked. Before he asked if I knew who he was, I nodded in response. I kept shaking my head. "I'm Diana's uncle.""Erin? Erin?" I heard my mom call my name on the line. I pointed to the phone and said, "Dad," he seemed to understand and turned to continue making pancakes.

"Huh. Um. Mum, Mr. Anderson is here. He's making breakfast. Sorry, I've been distracted?" I told her, smiling at Mr. Anderson, but his back was on me. He turned around just as she told him to talk.

"My mom wants to talk to you," I said, holding my phone. Once he took it, he wiped his hands on a towel. I took a seat in the bar stool on the island that was sitting in the middle of the kitchen. I saw Mr. Anderson talk on the phone with my aunt, running around the house, gathering things to make what looked like scrambled eggs. I've had a hard time believing it was Diana's brother. Granted, I barely paid attention to him when I saw him a couple of years ago, but I was damned. Now I just got weird. How many girls out there think that their dad's best friend was attractive? I don't think I've ever seen an elderly man before. My imagination didn't help me relax as it kept thinking where the happiness trail would lead or how hot his butt looked in the PJ pants. I must have slipped into dreamland while I was dreaming about him nude because the next thing I knew was that Mr. Anderson was waving his hand in front of my ear. I shook my head and went back to reality.

"Your mom just wants to make sure your stay is comfortable and I'm helping you move your stuff. She said to call her later because I told her that I'm going to feed you breakfast." He handed me my phone and told my plate that he had to fill up while I was dreaming.

"Thank you," I wrote. I just didn't know what else to say. He was a mysterious mystery to me, who happened to be Diana's brother, too. Yeah, I'm going to keep telling myself that she's her brother because it can't get any weirder.

"I'd like to apologize for not being here when you came last night. I had every intention of making sure that we had you checked in properly, but it seems that my staff can't handle a couple of hours alone without anything going wrong. I had to go to the office. But today, I switched off my work phone and told them I wouldn't be around. We should get you settled and make sure you're relaxed.

"It's all right, I understand you're running your own business. It's got to take a lot of time. Diana and I could use the help to get my things done. We thought if you weren't around, we'd have to pick up a hot guy to help us." I grinned as I took a bite of my meal and watched him raise his eyes.

"A hot guy, huh? I'm pretty sure a gorgeous girl like you wouldn't have any problems with that." He winked at me, "But I guess I'd rather help, I'm not sure any guy around here would be happy to just help you move, but they'd want more. This is California, baby, a whole new world compared to Omaha  that Diana tells me about." I don't know what it was, the wink, he's basically saying I'm beautiful, or c. His grin, too, didn't help much, such a beautiful smile that touched his lips.

"Well, Mr. Anderson, I don't think I'd bring in a man I've never met. Diana has a lot more luck in that area... getting the attention of the boys, I mean, not bringing home random guys," I quickly added the last bit because he looked shocked, I didn't want him to think his daughter was a slut, she wasn't at all. "And this place is completely different from home, but I feel like I'm going to settle down nicely. Thank you for allowing me to stay here. I'm very grateful because I know we don't know a lot about each other.""We're going to get to know each other over time. You're welcome here any time, even when you're done with school. You two have been friends forever, I'm never going to let you stop coming here. Did Diana give you the grand tour?

"She showed around the house, it was dark, so I couldn't see the back yard. She said there were an underground pool and a small pool house?" "There is also a tennis court by the yard which is used in hosting friends whenever there are special occasions,"  he said as I handed him my empty dish when he offered to take it.

"Why wouldn't you come with me, and I can give you a tour of the backyard?" he offered, holding his hand out to me. I picked it up and climbed off the bar stool. He taught me how to get to the back yard and the pool, which had a small hot tub attached to the end of it. He clarified that if he wanted to heat the whole room, but had never done it before, my mind immediately went to a small dive in the warm water, and the goosebumps formed on my shoulders. I hope he didn't realize that he hadn't let my hand go. I was curious if this would be considered odd by others if they could see it. He directed me to the pool house, which was like a small house with a mini kitchen and a seating area. There was a small room on the side of the house where pool tools and flotation gear were kept. He found out that the doors to the building could simply be wide open and that everything would be opened to the sea.

"I cleaned the pool when I got home in case you girls want to chill and swim today. Maybe after we get your things moved in?" he said.

"It might be a nice way to relax, but I didn't pack a bathing suit," I told him. He looked down at me, he seemed like his eyes were just skimming over my frame, I was still wearing an oversized shirt, he wasn't sure he could picture me a lot. My face felt wet and I looked away.

"I'm sure you can take care of that," he told me. I wasn't sure what he meant by that. Was that an innocent or a filthy remark? No, I think he was just being sweet to me and trying to make me feel at home. "Why don't we wake up Diana and get your stuff in your room?" he asked.

It's better to do it now if we wait, Diana won't wake up until late in the afternoon if we let her.""Oh, sure," I said with a slight change of subject. He let go of my hand and went back to the house.

I asked what that was about. Was there anything going on here, and I was right? Or was I mistaken, and the people of California were just strange?

I am still in the dreamland and thinking so hard about all that had happened. Whatever my final thoughts are, I think I'm going to find out...

# SEX WITH MY BEST FRIENDS' DAD

He was the first guy ever to get his dick to that spot in the back of my mouth, where it could slide down my throat. It was an exhilarating experience, discovering that there's a whole new thing out there to explore and do. I was shocked that no one had ever done this with me before, what I could infer from the fact that it seemed very common with guys, but they were too afraid to do it in real life, or at least to attempt it.

Most times, I think about if there is a thing that could make me unwind all that I had been through, especially in the hands of my best friend's dad, but each time this comes to my mind, I also remember not ready to let go of all the first scenarios he gave me while at his best.

My best college mate had a lake house about an hour away from our school. We would go there a couple of times a semester with our group of girlfriends and whatever guys we were dating/crusting at the moment to spend the weekend playing games and tempting each other to dive thin. It was a dream of college students.

I've seen her dad a couple of times since I've known her. I saw him the same day I saw her, lugging her heavy furniture into our freshman's room, exhausted and attractive — in a rough, masculine way. His name was Steve, and after packing up late that day, he bought a hamburger.

"Has anyone ever told you that your dad's very hot?" I asked when we went to bed that night, looking at a bit of a salacious problem that would tie us. "Haha, are you one of those girls? I don't get the whole" rich dad "thing. They're just old. I like them young." It was the last talk we had about him, but it wasn't the last time I thought of him. I always made sure I was going to dress my best because I realized he was coming by. Small skirts could only be worn by a college freshman, low-cut tank tops, and once — when I was especially bored — a sheer white T-shirt with no bra beneath because, "oh lawrd," I immediately moved out of bed.

It was a fun game to play, but I didn't think he'd ever noticed, or at least he'd never really recognized me until one of those wretched weekends when my friend and dad got their messages crossed and we all ended up at the lake house together. At first, when we arrived and saw the cars, Steve and his brother and some other people were there. They were organizing a fishing trip. Nevertheless, Steve gave us a nod and asked us to sit on the lower level and get out of our way. Everyone was pleased to tell my BFF the good luck of having a "cool" brother. But when Steve winked at us, I noticed something.

That night, after a lot of drinks, I found myself wandering out to the dock. Everyone else had passed away, but I was wide awake. I noticed Steve approaching me from the windy way down the hill from the cottage, two cold bottles in one hand. He handed me one wordlessly, scanning my mind for something — the reason I was awake and maybe alone.

We stood there quietly before he reached forward and swept my hair off my forehead, "You're a beautiful girl, Adrienne, don't think it's going to go unnoticed." I blushed, could he say I was having a crush on him? Did he notice the way I fucked his hand somewhat, uncertain about the strong reaction of my body to it?

"Thanks, Steve," I  uttered as I sip my bear with excitement while I looked up in the sky to the moon shining amazingly. As I dared to make eye contact with him again, I found that he hadn't moved, he was still studying me intently. Did that mean— before I could finish my thought, he was on me, one hand pressed very tightly on my lower back, the other in my hair as he kissed me. His tongue was in my mouth and I knew what was going on, circling mine. I had the desire to curl my legs around him, but there was nowhere to anchor this pier.

"Come up to my bedroom." It was a request, but it was also a statement, and he was sure of my answer.

When the threshold was crossed, I laughed and closed the back door. That was not all that he smiled and saw shadows under his lips, it wasn't just a physical attraction. It was his attitude, it was that he was a real living man, not a flimsy college boy. It was going to be a different kind of hook-up.

"You're married," I told him, not especially pleased to recall the fact.

"I will keep a secret," he said, closing his mouth again to mine, and moving us to the bunk.

He stripped all my clothing pretty quickly, and then he put it on top of me, fully clothed. The rough textures rubbing against my bare skin were unbelievable. "I can't believe this is going on," he said. "I've been doing this for a very long time.

I was trying to prove that I was worth it, all this harm. So I reached up and felt it through his pants, staring into his eyes longingly. He pulled his shirt over his head as I undressed, unzipped, and released a very healthy looking cock.

I slid off the bed and onto the floor to get a better angle, and he was standing over me, gathering my hair behind my head while I started to blast it. I looked up at him and was greeted with a smile that was most certainly in heaven as I took him in my mouth.

He was holding my head down on his cock while I was taking him deep inside. This was a gesture that was widely hated by every woman I met, but it was usually performed by dumb frat guys. Steve knew what he was doing, he was looking out for me and making the experience short — just long enough to add some excitement. He grinned as he backed out of me and bent down to kiss me. "I thought you were going to be very good at this." He pulled me up and headed over to a dresser underneath a large window.

I could still see the moonlight on the lake as it bent me over it. Was it just a few moments ago that we were almost strangers on the dock together? I was brought back to reality by Steve opening my thighs further apart and pressing my upper back down so my bare breasts were pushed to his smooth surface as I realized that he was penetrating me. "Oh my God..." I could help but scream as he crashed into me. He shocked me by pressing his hand over my mouth for a second as he was speeding up.

Obviously, my moan was too loud, but when he beat my ass many times and moaned and filled me with a cock, risking the loud sounds he made, he did not seem willing. I couldn't believe how this made me feel turned on. I wasn't a virgin, but I never had sex like this— it wasn't embarrassing or hasty. I was well aware that I was being fucked by a man, not "fooling around" with a boy.

"Are you on birth control?" he demanded, and when I answered yes, he cooed, "Good girl." The sound of that word coming out of his mouth pushed me across the brink, and I found myself squinting around his dick as I moved through my climax, still loving the sensation of a little extra liquid rolling down my leg.

He was still pushing me rhythmically, alternating between kneading my breasts and grabbing — and clapping— my ass. I haven't had sex this long yet, so I loved being able to enjoy the experience. "I'm getting closer," he groaned, and I tensed my back, keeping my position more tightly so that he could get farther inside of me as he poured his sperm into me. "You're very good at this, but I can tell you're just a beginner," he started as we lay down in his bed to relax.

It was true, I laughed. I had this fantasy of being a girl who gave a wonderful head and was really good at all the sex stuff, like some kind of woman fatale men couldn't resist. "But I can feel you want to learn." I nodded in agreement. I should play this crush and know what would motivate my next real wild boyfriend— who wouldn't want to kill the two birds with one stone?

And so, I started a year-long affair with Steve. We were going to sneak away for a weekend when I said I was visiting my parents and meeting at the lake house for lessons — how to stimulate differently for a long or short blow job, which positions let him get deep while still offering some kind of external stimulation for me, how to brace for and get anal, how to lie down with my head falling off the edge of the bed and let him move his dick. Occasionally, I just gave him my eyes while he was driving me around the campus, mindful not to drive anywhere too well-lit or occupied.

I never told my best friend about the sex, we would have stopped it when the passion went off at the end of the school year. At that point, I think we both got what we wanted from the relationship and had a life worthy of steamy sex. But every time I visit a lodge or a lake house, I can't help but think of the first night when he showed me so many possibilities.

# I DON'T WANT YOU TO HOLD ME BACK

Let me just say, with all the excitement that I can raise in my body, that this is my last year in high school. Well, it's the middle of the second semester, so I've got three more months or so before I'm finally home. Over the last four years, I've matured. I'm serious right now, I really have.

During my freshman year, I first started to wear make-up and stared at all the senior girls. That's where all my trouble began, in my new year. During my freshman, sophomore, and junior year, I've done a mess of things that I'm not particularly proud of right now: as a teenager, showing my tits to senior boys for $20, creeping into the boys ' room and smoking cigarettes, spraying a teacher's vehicle, and being called home several times  for wearing "inappropriate clothing."

But it was a different year. I've recently turned 18, and I haven't been in any serious trouble, I've played with most of my professors, I've been a tennis player, and for some reason, I've got damn good marks.

Our friend Jack had been living next door to us for years, and he knew all the problems I'd had in my first three years of high school. He must have noticed the screaming matches I had with my dad, and I'm sure that my mum, who had nothing else to do than a whisper, had gone to him moaning about what a difficult child I was. Throughout those years, any time I came across Jack, we'd talk a little bit about nothing in particular.

He was the only person I've never hated in those years. I know it was because he knew all my troubles, and yet he never talked about it — he never put me down, he never scolded me, he never talked to me like some grown-ups did, he never let me down, he never told me that I was tough and he wouldn't get "nowhere."

It was about 2:15 that afternoon, and I and the other girls on the tennis team got out of school early because we had a tennis match at Redwood High School, which was about half an hour away.

I went downstairs to the girls' locker room and turned into my tennis uniform, a white tennis skirt, and a white polo shirt. Our skirts were the type (of course) of white panties sewn into them, to slide over our real panties. "Bloomers" we called them because when our pleated skirts rose, it seemed like we were a "blooming" tree.

Several girls took the bus when we were out-of-town, while some of us were driving our own cars. Personally, I didn't have a choice in the matter. My condition was this: the gas prices in our town were high - about $3.75 per gallon and my vehicle had an empty tank. I've had about a week and a half to apply to my next paycheck. So to sum it up, I had to walk or depend on my parents everywhere I had to go to my next paycheck. Of course, in this situation, I'm going to take the school bus to Redwood.

The other girls surrounded me in the locker room, dressing and undressing, chatting and talking and the like. My aunt Kate was dressing next to me, pulling her skirt/bloomer hybrid over her underwear, chatting to me about her boyfriend Justin. Yeah, it's more like talking about Justin. He told me why I didn't have a boyfriend and what had happened to her-his-name a while ago.

"Amy," I replied, exasperated. "Two months ago, Jake and I broke up. Right now, I'm just taking a break from guys.""I know, and that's cool and it's all," she said. "But aren't there guys that you even want to go out with?""No one that I would really date," I replied.

"What do you mean?""Alright," I grinned. "I have a thing for Mr. Bradley.""Mr. Bradley! The calculus teacher? Ugh!" she exclaimed. "But he's, like, tired and nasty! "I smiled and he said, "not to me!" We burst out laughing a little, then we hastily finished getting dressed. By that time, many of the girls had come out of the locker room and hopped on the bus or in their cars. Kate said she was going to the bus. I told her I was going to meet her out there, I just had to use the bathroom really fast.

As I cleaned the tub, I found that the locker room was completely quiet and that everyone else had already left. I rushed out into the locker room, washed my hands quickly, gathered my book bag and tennis racket and raced out to the front door of the classroom just in time to see the school bus speeding down the highway.

"Grrrr!" I screamed, slamming down my racket. I missed the plane. What was I going to do now? I didn't have a choice but to walk half a mile backward. I didn't bother to change my tennis shirt, because it was one of the few clean clothes I still had, so I groaned again, remembering that I'd have to do a big pile of dirty laundry when I got home.

It was a very good day in mid-March, so I went out to the porch to do my homework after tossing my clothes into the washing machine. I put on the porch swing reading some stupid story about some crazy fight in a stupid war that we waged centuries ago. As I saw a car door close-by, I was trying to finish my reading assignment without nodding off. I shook my head to see who it was. I figured it was too early in the day for my parents to be at home. Instead, I saw Jack, who just turned into his driveway next door. Happy with the diversion, I headed over to see what he was up to.

"Hi, Jack!" I waved as I came to him.

"Hi Elizabeth Anne," he said, creating a grin. He looked like he was feeling awful. He looked sadder than anything else.

I gently touched his bare arm with my hand, "What's wrong with you, Jack?""Ugh," he groaned. "This is my birthday. Damn it, I just get older and older. I don't want to be cranky with you, Elizabeth Anne. It's just a hassle.""Yeah," I said quietly. "I'm sorry. Aw, I  made a cake some days ago. It's not necessarily a birthday cake or anything, but would you like a piece of cake?" He chuckled, "Elizabeth Anne, that would be great. I had a bad day at work, and this birthday thing just made things worse.""Okay, come inside," I grinned. I took him across our lawn and up the stairs to the house. We went to the kitchen. "You're sitting right there," I said, referring to the chair at the bar.

"Thank you so much, Elizabeth Anne, that's so cool," he said, taking the seat I offered.

"It's no problem. What would you like to drink? We've got milk, cola, lemonade, and tea.""I'm going to take a coke, thank you," he said.

I took the cake out of the oven and cut out a big slice of it and placed it on one of our best dishes. I think it's fair to say I liked Jack. I'd call it a feeling of affection for him. My very low desire for him was nearly imperceptible. It was not a thought of being madly in love or anything like that.

I poured a Sprite into a bottle of ice cubes, grabbed a fork and a pair of napkins, and carried his lunch out to the dining room where he was seated.

"Here you go," I said, bringing it in front of him.

He smiled at me with a grin, "Thank you so much, Elizabeth Anne. This kind of kindness sure helps an old man feel good." I replied with a gesture of my hand and took a seat next to him, "Don't be dumb. I don't think you're old at all.""Did you know how old I am?" I hesitated, "Yeah, no... but you're not behaving or looking old.""You want to guess?" he said with a laugh. "Something you say can't make me look any worse.""Well, I think maybe 40 or 41?" I said, "Almost," he replied. "Today I turned 45." 45, in my opinion, was not old at all. And I told him that. I've always had an attraction to older men-this, of course, I didn't tell him. I observed him in a very subtle way as he enjoyed his coffee. He was also quite odd. His subtle ugliness was on the brink of perfection. I've never been so close to him before, so I thought he'd be even better off looking up there, so I felt a little squirmy sitting next to this older man. He loved me; even if it was platonic, he liked me. And I was delighted with this. He commented on my tennis outfit and wondered if I was just getting back from school.

"Well," I said. "Our squad had a tennis match in Redwood, so I missed the bus. My car is pretty much destroyed. When I get my next paycheck, I'll be able to fix it up. It doesn't matter if I skipped the match. I'm not very successful anyway." He shook his head, "Now that, I'm sure you're definitely wrong. I know when you hit the ball back and forth with your friends out on the street— Then, he looked down into my eyes and into my lips. It looked like he was going to kiss me. Looking at his empty plate, I asked him if he was all finished, and he broke our moment together. I cursed myself secretly for wasting such a sensual moment.

I took the plate and the bottle and put it in the sink. I was seated next to him again, and we continued our talk. Somehow, we got to talk about our dating lives. I explained my condition to him, and he admitted to me that he never seemed to have dated.

"I asked a woman out a couple of weeks ago," he said bitterly. "Then she turned me down.""Why did she do that?" I asked, sounding indignant at the thought.

He glanced at me, shocked, and then said, "She said she didn't respect what I did for a living. " He said, tossing his eyebrows with a grin.

"Oh, not all women are fascinated with the life of a guy," I said, putting my hand on his shoulder closest to me. He looked down at my hand and then back at me. "Just a little new, are we?" he asked in a quiet voice.

"Would you want that?" I asked.

"No, not at all," he said.

My eyes just looked at him a mile a minute. I was gazing into his head. I have seen a sense of desire, but also of terror. I decided to move very slowly as if to give him a chance to pull away if he needed to. I moved my chair closer to him and turned my head very softly, my lips close to him, he showed me no hint that he wanted me to stop. And I bent more and brushed my soft lips to his. Our lips remained closed for a minute, but I was shocked when he took the initiative and opened his mouth to me, softly taking my face in his big hands.

I loved the feeling that I was next to him, his face so close to mine. One thing I liked doing was nibbling and licking a man's neck. So obviously, my lips moved away from him and down to his face, where I kissed my nose and started to kiss him. I heard him groan and I realized that he weaved his fingertips through my curly head of blond hair.

"Oh, Elizabeth Anne," he yelled. "Wait, wait, we can't go on like that." I pulled away, disappointed. "Why not?""Elizabeth Anne," he replied, a matter of fact. "I'm 45. You're just 18. That's just not the right thing to do. I feel like I'm taking advantage of you.""But I'm the one who made the first move," I replied.

He stood up, "I know, I know. Well, we really can't do that. I'm sorry, Elizabeth Anne." He placed his chair gently under the table and stepped into the living room, walking through the front door.

I was sitting there, feeling so confused. If I was too young, why did he let me kiss him first? I've given him a lot of opportunities to get away from my advances. I just didn't know what to say about it. I wasn't angry-I couldn't be upset at Jack. I was grateful, in a way, that he had put a stop to things. It proved that he was a gentleman and that he actually took my youth into account. Personally, I think I felt disappointed.

The next morning, I woke up (I love it when that happens) and felt a feeling of dread coming over me when I realized I was going to have to walk past Jack's house to get to school. Of all the time that my car was going to be bone dry, I thought to myself, shaking my head. How shameful, not to throw myself at an older man, but to be thrown under the bus by this older man! My feeling was one of anger that morning. I became furious that he had refused me. Sad that he did not see me mature enough and old enough to be deserving of his love

I got up and put on my little white cotton shorts, my 34b white bra, and a white T-shirt in my hair. Eventually, I pulled on a pair of denim daisy duke shorts. One thing I liked about my hair is to bring the sides back to the middle of my head and tie it with a bow. I picked a blue baby bow this morning and washed my hair and put it in place. I brushed my teeth and went downstairs.

As I came down, my dad had already gone to work, and my mom was sleeping in, as it was her day off. I made a quick breakfast for myself, then I went to school.

Once outside, I found that Jack's car was still in his driveway. Damn. Damn. I wanted to go hard, but my plan failed when I heard Jack's screen door open. I dismissed him, so I kept walking past his house. I could hear his feet behind me, nearly jogging, and he jumped in front of me, halting my trip.

"Elizabeth Anne, let's talk about it yesterday," he said, looking down at me with such a saddened look on his face.

I looked up at him in rage, "What's to think about? You clearly don't like me, and that's all there's to it." He looked offended by my tone. "Elizabeth Anne, of course, I like you. Our kiss would never have happened if I didn't like you." I stared at him with a confused expression. She seemed as puzzled as I might have felt at him. He just seemed to be too confused. Yesterday, our kiss tore up his soul, and now he's standing here, professing his love for me? I didn't know what to say or do about it.

His words have taken the place of my confusion. "You're one of the prettiest, sweetest girls I've ever met. Can I see you again?" he said quietly.

My confused mouth unwrinkled, and I grinned at him and nodded. He softly tucked my hair behind my ear, keeping my face in his hands. His eyes were not leaving mine. He spun 100 feelings in his lap. There was guilt, lust, longing, confusion, and conflict. But he gave in to the most powerful, tilted his head and leaned down to kiss me. My hand shot up to his neck and held him back to his head. I played my fingertips with his soft, dark hair, the nails painted in pink. We opened our mouths to each other, and I was whimpering with pleasure.

He pulled away and said, "I don't want to make you late for school. It's actually pretty hot. Can I take you to school?" I giggled, "That would be awesome. You don't know how sick I'm driving!" He chuckled, "I can imagine!" He left the passenger door open for me and I got in. He simply went into the car by the driver's seat and ignited the car.

We were talking a bit about tennis, as he was on his tennis team when he was in high school and other tennis-related stuff. I felt flattered that he was going to open that part of his life to me, even if it was something as impersonal as tennis. I moaned and moaned at him as to how I'd never been a very good player, and how my tennis skills suckled.

"I just don't seem to get the hang of the forehand," I whined. "And my service-well, we're not going to do that for now.""It's just a game," he said. "What's really going on doesn't matter at all, but you know, I have to say, I've been itching to get back to the sport myself for the last couple of years.""Why haven't you?" I replied, smiling at him. He looked so nice as he was walking, the sunshine playing on his forehead, the grin he wore when we were chatting.

"Yeah, with work and everything, it's been hard to squeeze it in. I haven't had to work that much though recently. I'm still feeling pretty burnt out and my manager cut my hours a little bit. I'm enjoying having a little more free time." He hesitated, "Elizabeth Anne, may I recommend something?""Sure.""Okay, I know you want to improve your game, and here I am and I want to get back into the ga. "How does that strike you?" I grinned widely, "I'd love that!""So I'd say, why don't I give you my phone number? You can call whenever you want, and if I'm not home, you can always leave a message." I blushed, "I-I'd like that a lot, Jack." He started searching his wallet for some kind of paper he could put his phone number on. I opened my book bag, opened my book on page 223, and handed him a pad. "Here, you can just write in my diary," he said, "Yeah, that sounds good. I don't want them to make you pay for the damage though.""Alright, it'll be all right, they'll never know the difference." I closed my book and put it back into my book bag with my pad. I stood there, nervously, for a minute, until I remembered that I didn't have too much time to be uncomfortable because I was nearly late for my first lecture. I gave him a hug and a shy kiss on the cheek, and I thanked him for the ride. I got out and knocked at the door, walking up the steps of my school.

Right after lunch, I had a physics class, which I thought was my most boring lesson. So it wasn't shocking to me when Jack came into my head and I started thinking about him. Very explicitly, I might add that. I was astounded by my feelings, for although I had always had a slight crush on him, my thoughts on him had never been so raw and erotic. I dreamed that he was sitting on a sofa and unzipping his slacks so that I could ride him wildly like an athlete. I spontaneously began to put his name in my diary, with the hearts around it. In the school-girlishness of my actions, I almost giggled out loud.

Kate, who was across the aisle from me, must have noticed me squirming and passed me a note that read, "You're wiggling like a worm! You've got your mind on something?" And I realized how short a time it took me to fall for Jack. I saw him as the good guy next door two days ago. But what had happened over the past day, and the kisses we shared, made me realize that I cared for him and valued him more than I realized.

I ripped out a sheet of paper to write a note back to Kate, that read, "Well, I do not want to offer you so much info, but I can still use a dry pair of panties right now!" Then, with my horrid timing, the teacher noticed me tossing my note across the hallway then scolding me. Then she took out the yellow paper pad that I knew so well. After a moment, she pulled off the top sheet and ordered me to go to the front of the room and read the cover. Tomorrow, at 3 o'clock sharp, I was going to be in the detention room for 30 minutes of copying the school rules.

And so the end of the day arrived, and my detention was in session, and it was over early, so I glanced out one of the windows and saw that it was raining hard. Suddenly, I remember that Jack had given me his phone number. I went to my locker to find his number, and I called him on my cell phone. After a few rings, he picked up the phone.

"Hello?""Hi Jack, it's Elizabeth Anne.""Hey, Elizabeth Anne, what's going on?""Nothing much. I was wondering if you're not busy or anything, maybe you could pick me up at school? It's raining so hard and I'm still stuck here because I was in custody." He said it wouldn't be a problem. I thanked him for that, and we hung up.

I was waiting at the front doors of the academy. A few minutes later, his car was pulling in the lot. I opened the door and raced to his car in the rain. I fell into the passenger seat, shuddering.

He gave me a nice look, "Aw, here, I'm going to turn the heat up." He fiddled with the dials in his car, and it soon got warmer. We headed home.

"Thank you for taking me up, I really appreciate it," I said, smiling over at him.

"Oh, that's no problem," he said in a squeak of a voice. He was acting out a little bit.

"Are you all right?" I told him.

"Y-yes, I'm all right." There was definitely something going on in his head. But what has changed since this morning? Nothing I could think of. Then it was dawning on me. I looked down at my soaked T-shirt and saw that my nipples poked suggestively from my waist.

"Oh, my gosh," I said, smiling. "I'm so sorry. I didn't realize that I was so, you know, open," he said, "It's no problem." He pulled into his driveway, almost wiping the fence in the process. "I know you're just living next door and everything, but would you like to come in?" he asked. I looked into his brown eyes, "Yeah." I grinned.

We braved the storm and opened our doors. We started to run to his front door, but the poor sweetheart slipped into some mud and put his face in the dirt. He laughed so hard, and I smiled at how much he felt like a wet dog. I helped him to his feet, and we ran to his house, still laughing at his little mishap.

"Huh," I smiled at him. "You're so clumsy!" he laughed, barely able to catch his breath, "Oh, I laugh so hard that my stomach hurts!""Me too!" I giggled.

Our laughter was simmering in silent giggles, and we stood there looking at each other for a moment. It seemed so normal that I could fall into his embrace. He stayed still for a moment, and then he slithered his arms around my soaked body. I looked up at him, and we hugged him passionately. The rain clapping on the pavement outside, the crackling of the bricks. He caressed the surface of my messy, wet hair as we kissed, and now my bow was loose and unorganized. He broke our kiss and looked down at me.

"You're the most precious thing I've ever seen," he whispered.

I looked up at him, his eyes were watery from his sincerity. We grasped each other's hands, squirmed nervously, and I had no doubts about what I wanted to say.

"Today, I've been thinking so much about you," I said.

"Yeah, I was worried about you too."

We parted and stepped into the living room. He ignited the fireplace, and soon the flames went up. He took a seat on the couch, and I was right beside him. I was eager to continue our dating, and he had the same thing in mind as soon as we were excited about it. I moved toward him to plant a kiss on him as I was sitting with my leg leaned backward.

His hand rested on my hip, and when I didn't object, his hand slithered upward, and he began to caress my neck. It made me very excited, and I began to unbutton his shirt, kissing the spot where every button had been.

"Damn," he groaned. "Are you sure of this Elizabeth Anne?""I'm sure," I said softly as I slipped his shirt over his shoulders. His chest was beautiful. His face was wet with the heat, and he had a beautiful coat of chest hair.

He asked if he could take my top off. I was eagerly in agreement and raised my arms as he peeled it away from me, the cotton hugging my wet skin. Immediately, I started to unbuckle his belt, and he started kissing me again, and very subtly, he undressed my bra, which stuck to my pointed tits. I slid off his shirt, and a moment later, my arm was on the cement.

I told him to stand up and take off his coat, socks and shoes. He agreed, and he was about to sit back down when I told him to stay. I stood up, took off my shorts and panties, unclipped my bow and knelt in front of him. His cock was very good. It was thick and 6-7 inches long. This was long and difficult for me to believe especially taking all of it in me. I opened my eyes and started taking as much of it as I could in my mouth.

He groaned loudly and twisted his hand in my hair. I looked up at him, his head tilted back, his eyes closed in satisfaction. "Damn," he moaned. "Suck me, sweetheart." Encouraged by his words, I sucked him more aggressively. "That's boy, oh my, when did you learn to do that? You and that little tongue of yours." Then, I could feel him looking down at me, and I smiled at him slowly and seductively, my eyes sleepy in my lust for him, which I knew would quickly erupt.

He softly pulled his dick out of my mouth and told me to lie down on the floor. I did what he said. My body was completely naked in front of him. He couldn't stop staring at my nude ass. He kneeled down and spread his thighs softly.

"My, my," he said when he saw my cunt. I knew what I felt like when my legs were open because I used a mirror to my full advantage a few weeks ago. He noticed my tiny clit click. My pink teen pussy folds spread wide for him. Slick wetness, begging for some kind of attention. And so it had been given.

He started licking my pussy gently, licking my juices like a kitten. He opened my lips and dug as far as he could into my pit. I was moaning and crying, pushing my slit into his greedy mouth. I humped his jaw as hard as I could, but I needed so much more than a kiss. He nibbled at my clit.

"Oh, Christ," I groaned. "Oh, oh, Jack, feed me, eat my cunt," he breathed. "This is a sweet little crack." He then sat down on his knees and dragged my body towards him very delicately. He took his big dick in his hand and kissed my girl's folds with his cock's ass. I spread my legs wide, giving him an open invitation.

At first, he sank the head of his dick into my pussy very gently. He looked at me and asked if I was okay. I was gripping the carpet under us, and I said I was begging him for more. He slowly came in, searching my face for any indication that he was supposed to stop. What I needed was his cock in me. Soon every inch of his virility had sunk inside my body, and I sighed with satisfaction.

"Yeah," I moaned. "Give it to me.""You want some more, precious?" he asked. "Oh yeah, give me some." He picked up his pace and started to fuck me. "Oh please Jack," I whispered. "Come on, quicker, deeper." And he was soon going to fuck me fast and hard, without guilt or excuse. Just the way I expected him to do it. I opened my eyes, and I saw how manly he felt, driving all his meat into me, raping me. God, how much I used to fuck.

"Damn, oh yeah," I said. "Oh, fuck me so hard Jack. Come on, come on." Between his groans, he was able to ask if I was on birth control. I said no, and he said he was going to pull out before he walked in. I nodded, only half-understanding what he said. I was so much more interested in his dick, and in the way, he was fucking me. My breasts jiggled with every inward stroke.

"Oh, Jack!" I squealed. "I'm cumming!" and not a moment later, I heard my little cunt throb like a rhythm around his steel-hard fucker He groaned, "Holy fuck! Fuck, I can't take it anymore, Elizabeth Anne." And he pulled out and straddled my stomach to spray his cum on my breasts.

"Oh, yeah," I moaned. "Cum on my boobs.""You like that sweetheart?" he said as he snapped in front of me. "You like all that nice sperm on your little body?" I nodded, biting my bottom lip. He squirted his sperm a moment later. His goo was heavy, so he flew over my breasts, a drop of it settling on my chin and mouth. He dribbled out a little more sperm and was done. I licked the cum close to my lips and started to rub in the cum that was on my breasts.

He reached for a pair of pillows on the sofa and eased one under my head while sitting on the other. We've both been pants tight from our orgasms, not really revealing too much of anything. After a few minutes, his cum was dry and I snuggled up to him.

"Mmm, sweetheart," he moaned. "You're such a hot mess," I said.

We had been sitting in silence for a few more minutes, so he proposed he get a shower for us. I nodded as I came down from the heat of my orgasm, and I began to feel chilly because of the cold, damp air and the fact that I was naked on the floor.

He went down the hallway and into the bathroom, beginning with a hot shower. A minute later, I stood up and joined him. I walked into the shower, and he greeted me with a smile.

"That felt so good," I said.

"It really did," he said. "I haven't made love in more than three years."

I giggled as we dried each other up, kissing each other's faces. He washed my hair because of me. The shower was sensual but rather brief, and we went out and dried each other out. His hand caressed my body with a towel, and his touch was so soft and so caring. He wrapped his towel around his waist and gave me his huge, fluffy bathrobe to wear. This went down to my knees, and I felt so elf-like that I was bundled up.

I was sitting on the couch and he picked up our clothes and stormed into the laundry room, tossing them in the dryer. I fished in my purse, found my shampoo, and began to wash my hair. I led him to the back of the house, wondering if he had a hairdryer. She said there was one underneath the washbasin after his sister had visited him for Christmas. I went into the bathroom and plugged it in, drying my head. It's been a heck of an afternoon, the most fun I've ever had.

Three days later, on Saturday, the sun was shining and I found myself in my high school court, up against a high school rival in the nearby town of Kingsville. This girl from Kingsville was great. Our tennis teams played the best of three sets, and I took the first set at 6-3. I had one set under my belt, but I was challenging my concentration when Jack was in the stands. When would I have been able to concentrate?

Clearly, what's happened over the last few days has made him my husband. And he told me how proud he was that I was his girlfriend. We were caring about each other, and the relationship we seemed to pledge would always be steamy and safe.

After a grueling second set under the heat, the second set was officially declared mine and I won. The kid and I met in the sea and shook hands.

The last set was suspenseful and very long, and at this point Jack was standing on the side of the stalls, leaning against the chain-link fence. He was smiling brightly in my direction, and I dropped my racquet and ran over to him.

"Thanks for being here with me today, Jack," I hugged him close. I said, panting from the match.

"You've done so well today, sweetheart, I'm so proud of you." I giggled and ran back to the tennis court section, picking up my racket, gym bag, canteen, and towel. I screamed to Jack that I'd only be a couple of minutes late, that I had to go to the locker room to take a shower. He smiled quite cleverly.

I stood under the hot steam of the locker room shower and thought about how fortunate I was to be with such a wonderful man. He was sweet, caring, kind, funny, and extremely sexy and sexy.

Happy to be out of the hot sun, and happy to be finished with my shower, I took my time to dry. The towel around my neck, I washed my hair and cleaned it vigorously, bringing the curls back away from my face in my custom Elizabeth cap.

One final day, I washed and put on a new pair of panties and a tank, pulling out a pair of shorts and a top of my gym bag. My shorts were denim, and my top was a delicate baby pink thing, with the puffy sleeves on it hugging my shoulders. Eventually, I attached a bracelet that Jack had given me the day before.

I approached Jack outside in the stands, and he asked me if I was all ready for a big meal. I nodded eagerly, saying that I was famished.

We were seated in the restaurant booth, side by side. Each of us had our own glass of Coke, and we snuggled close to each other, waiting for our meal.

"You were just a beautiful sweetheart," he said to me. "Thanks, Jack," I glanced over and grinned at him.

"And," he said, beginning to kiss my face. "You looked lovely." He lowered his mouth to my ear and whispered, "I always loved the way your tiny ass looked in those blossoms, sweetheart. If your skirt would fly up, my cock would be so hard." I giggled, "It would be?""Oh yes," he said to me, almost groaning.

"Yeah, it was a tough tennis match, but I also think you deserve a break for staying in that sun for so long.""Oh yeah?" he said to me, his arm around me, looking down at me with a grin.

I took his hand and led him down a small hallway to the men's bathroom. It wasn't a bathroom with a variety of rooms, it was just a small room with a toilet and a shower, and so on. I closed the bathroom door behind us and knelt in front of him, desperately unbuckling his belt, his dick so hard and wanting to get rid of his prison.

I took down his pants and panties in one of the tugs, and his cock stuck out, so erect and eager.

"Before I blast you," I said sexily to him. "I want you to know that you're free to fuck my mouth at any time.""Fuck," he whispered.

I started kissing his cock and spread my lips to him, putting the head of his cock in my mouth. After a few minutes, his horniness took over, taking my face in his hands, pounding my ass. His hot, slick dick plunged in and out of the space between my legs, begging for release. I gagged on his dick a couple of times, but it was worth it.

He grunted with every line, "Uh... uh... uh... uh."

It wasn't long for him to cum. He spurred his sperm all over, and I was able to catch most of it in my hand. I could feel the long streams of goo relaxing down my throat. I gulped everything he had to offer, and after he was done, he giggled his softening cock between my lips. I cleared some of them and took a shower slowly.

We approached the table, food was sitting there, waiting for us to swallow it. But our appetites were already satisfied.

# THE DAD OF HER CLOSEST FRIEND

Peter's first thought was, "What is it?"

The website wasn't strictly legal, it was basically an online brothel, often visited since you married and separated in high school, and the children were a bit independent. He didn't mean he couldn't get the date if he wanted, but he didn't. Too much work without a certain reward. The website offered him exactly what he wanted at night and knew they were pretty-brunette or blonde, kinky or vanilla big boobs, or little ones. There was a branch in another place and he was fortunate to be able to live an hour away from one of them.

He had a child this week, so he decided to check the website to see if he had something to know.

There was a boy.

He, of course, immediately recognized her. She spent almost as many weekends at his home as his daughter spent the past year. If he remembers correctly, he turned 18 last month. At that time all the talk was about her birthday party.

5'4 "petite, short blond hair brushing shoulders, glowing green eyes, high breasts probably between B and C cups, small waist, and a bright smile indicating that she is a cheerleader.

Emily Walters, his daughter's best friend from high school first grade.

Sell her virgin on the Internet

The bid was open until midnight.

If he was another kind of man, he might have bid to save her from her. Save her from what she thought she was doing. However, he noticed over the years that he did not care what stupid decisions others had made without affecting him or his children. Why do you need him? And at least he will be a better choice for her than many other guys on this site. He knew that she looked good and that women of all ages would be attractive even if they were on the other side of the age of forty. Unlike his ex-husband, he remained fit after his marriage, but he went to the gym several times a week and ran regularly. Once or twice he even whispered that his daughter's friend had a hot dad on her.

And he wasn't going to hurt Her, not more than he had to. He would have made it perfect for her.

Fortunately, he had a lot of money since the divorce was more or less accommodating when it came to economics, and they both had high salaries. They'd agreed to split it up fairly equally, and he'd never needed to pay for the child's home, although of course, he'd played his part for the kid's college, he'd set up a fund for that a long time ago.

So he's got a lot of money to spend if he wants to... And that's what he wanted to waste it on.

Two hours later, an almost absurd amount of money, he was the proud owner of teenage virginity. He put all the relevant information on when / where to meet this coming weekend in the form given by the website.

Hotel Windham, room no 105

Emily almost licked her lips out of nervousness before she remembered she was wearing lipstick. Was she really going to do that?

Sure, sure.

Not because of the money, even though that ridiculously high amount was a nice bonus. This was something she had been preparing for a long time since she heard from the website that she had auctioned her virgin. Almost exactly a year ago, she had heard her older sister talk to one of her friends about it; her friend used it as a dating service, but she said the best money went to the virgin.

The people who used this site were very rich and had their ages on the high side, by that I mean mature: very mature.

She'd always had something to do with older men, bullying her teachers all over the high school, her parents, just about anyone older. Even if they weren't hot or in great shape, she found them so much more intriguing than the boys of her age. Which was how she was to become the only virgin in the cheerleading squad, boys just didn't care about her age.

But to surrender her virginity to an elderly man, a stranger, huh For some excuse, her jets were getting hot and ready. Maybe reality isn't going to live up to the dream, but at least she'd be well rewarded for missing her hymen. None of her mates were still in friendship with the man who popped up their cherry, so they didn't get anything out of the conversation like it was.

She took a deep breath and adjusted the collar of the skimpy white sundress she was wearing and inserted the hotel key into the door.

The skirt of her dress was spinning around her legs when she walked through the door. The hotel room was almost spotless, but across the floor, there was a guy sitting in a chair staring out at the glass. Since none of the lights were on, she couldn't see any of his faces, only his silhouette against the glare of the glass as he rose and turned to her. He was tall, had a healthy hair crop and looked pretty nice, but that was all she could see.

Anticipation and involuntary lust tingled in her body as she put a faint laugh on her face and stepped forward, shutting the door behind her. Was it her imagination, or could her eyes love care for her young body and actually feel the low cut on the front of her halter dress and the skirt across her tanned thighs?

"Hello," she replied, unnerved by his absence and doing her best to cover it up. "I'm Emily, you've got to be Paul." She flicked at the light switch and screamed. "Oh my god... Mr. Davids?!" Mary's dad's familiar handsome face was the last thing she'd expected to see. A rather rugged profile, surrounded by dark hair with a hint of gray at the temples, and little silvery highlights sprinkled throughout the piece of scruff on his chin. Mr. Davids was a DILF, Dad I'd love to fuck. It was a running joke among his daughter's friends. Oh, in the summer she'd drooled over him wearing a swimsuit. She would sign at him when he did something particularly nice or caring for the girls. Masturbated multiple times to the vision of him in his mind

However, she has not been completely humiliated by daydreaming as it is now.

The vision of being with an older, rich, mature man immediately appeared filthy and frail as she looked at the guy she met... That she had known for years and knew what she knew she had lost her virginity on the market. She was feeling disgusting. Ashamed, man. Impossibly young and stupid, If she was fortunate, he'd just mock her and not tell her parents what she'd done. And she'd have to give him the money back, of course. Lord, Father... Why did she cover the amount that the website took?

Her cheeks bloomed crimson, paling to silver, several times as he stood there studying her, It's testing her. Tears of humiliation aroused in her eyes.

"I can't imagine what you have to say of me," she whispered, lowering her head to the floor, not having to see the disappointment and judgment on her forehead.

"I think... that right now you look more beautiful than ever before," he said quietly in his dark, oh-so sexy voice. "And I've been looking forward to this all week." Shock suffocated her, so her head flew back when she realized that he was coming towards her. There was something she had never seen before in her dark eyes, and she felt a burning feeling deep in her belly as her body responded to it. As some primal impulse in her brain said that the guy in front of her desired her... Wanted her to...

"Are you... are we..." he couldn't have said...

"What's the matter, Emily?" he demanded, his deep voice fluttering in a way that made her heart relax, her hair pressing on the back of her neck. He stopped moving towards her, standing at the foot of the bed, and she realized that she couldn't stop looking at the piece of furniture she had thought she was losing her virginity. That she might lose her virginity if her instincts were correct. "Do you have any second thoughts about selling your virginity?" And that she was curious if he was just trying to scare her. Twisting her hands in front of her, she tried to figure out her thoughts, she tried to think about something to say, but she felt like she was flying across space at top speed, and in a second she was going to crash, because there was nothing she could do to slow herself down or stop her, and there was no fresh oxygen to yell a lot less chat. Worse still, she could feel aroused by the idea of losing her v-card to Mr. David Heck, uh... He was so soft. Older than that. The disparity between him and the boys of her age was hilarious.

"You know what I'm thinking?" his voice was like a caress over her face, and he was stepping towards her again. It's sluggish. It's deliberate. Her muscles were tight, shouting at her to run, but she couldn't move right now if her life depended on it. "I thought you wanted to do something a little crazy, to lose your virginity to a man who knows what he's doing, who can make you feel something..." He stood right in front of her and raised his finger to her jawline and began to run it down her neck, down the center of her collar bone and down to her cleavage. It felt like her nipples were polished diamonds, and she felt her breathing constricted as her finger started to trace the low-cut neckline of her sundress. The eyes of Mr. Davids never left her. "A guy who can make sure you enjoy it."

Then, when he slit her breast in his warm hand, Emily moaned and almost slumped in front of him. Okay, it feels so... Nice. Good. He wasn't the first man to touch her breast, but he was certainly the first man. It was a completely different experience to have Mr. Davids feels her up. The suddenness of his hold on her soft flesh, the fire of his eyes, his utter confidence as he kissed her, was nothing like the puffy, vain boys she had made out with, in the backs of their cars. She moaned with anticipation from the sight of her breasts, groaned without finesse, and she didn't feel a tenth as enthusiastic as she was right now.

His eyes were all on hers without blinking, Mr. David raised his other hand so that he could gently squeeze both of her breasts, and she panted as she felt the fabric of her dress rubbing against her nipples. The sundress didn't allow for a bra, so she didn't wear one.

The expression on his face did not change, although he could swear that his eyes looked more tired and hungry. And, all of a sudden, his hands were gone, and she was left standing crying as he turned his back and walked away.

Sudden fear has assailed her. What did she do wrong?

Mr. David turned and sat on the bed in front of her. "Take off your dress Emily, I want to see what I paid for." Her entire body was heated by a flush, along with a healthy dose of frustration. He kept referring to her as if she was a... Her eyes were pink. She was like a slut who sold her body for money.

Which is exactly what she did, he waited patiently, watching her with that hollow look as she raised her head, turning her neck to loosen the zipper. Her throat felt incredibly dry, and she knew she was anxious. Because she was trying to find him attractive, how strange it was that she suddenly felt so incredibly uncertain about herself, but he would have put her off balance by talking to her the way he did.

Her hands trembled even more as she tugged down the straps of her dress and unveiled her almost completely naked body to her best friend's dad. The person who paid her just for taking her virgin

"Panties," he muttered, her eyes crossed her curve, and she wanted to curse him. I want more replies from him. Nevertheless, her nipples continued to throb and her woman creamed her underwear as if she were really treated this way.

Nearly defiantly, Emily pulled her panties away from her waist and let them slip along with her top, exposing her neatly trimmed pussy. It had only a tiny patch of blonde pubic hair surrounding her, and she had absolutely shaved her pussy lips beneath. Unable to hold Mr. David's gaze in her nude and vulnerable state, Emily dropped her head as she gasped, noticing that she was staring at a very big penis at the front of her trousers.

Not awkward at all, Mr. David just smiled when he knew where she was going.

"Don't worry sweetheart, I'm trying to be soft." It was meant to be cliché. It was supposed to sound dumb. Then, she just found herself shivering with excitement. It's with fire.

"Come over." Emily, shutting her eyes for a moment, collected her courage. Once she opened them again, Mr. David was still sitting on the bed staring at her, a thin, somewhat threatening grin decorating his mouth. Her hands twisted as she took a step forward. The smile of Mr. David was widening and she felt her breath stuttering. Feeling like she was going toward the edge, positioning herself for a freefall, Emily kept walking until she was standing right in front of Mr. Davids. The echo of her heart's pounding flooded her ears.

When he put his hand between her feet and brushed his fingers between her fluffy virgin pussy lips, she put his eyes on her face and she gasped Was. Emily's face was warm and unbearable, her eyes closed and her fingertips shook looking for her body entrance.

"Please..." he asked, "Please, what?" one long finger pushed inside her and gasped.

She covered her face with her hands, unable to stop a soft sigh from coming out of her mouth. "Please, this is so embarrassing... can't you just do it?" Mr. David laughed, the sound so dark and rich that it made her shudder as she glanced at him through her fingers. She did not realize that her hesitation, her honesty, the very sincerity of her appeal was turning him on even more. What she knew was that her best friend, DAD, was waiting for her in this room, not putting her hands between her thighs and expecting her to pierce her with fingers and penetrate

"Oh lover, I'm not going to do anything, that's what a child who can't control his emotions, because you wanted a man." But he said he was in danger. I knew. After all, he wanted this to be comfortable for her, but now his body lay on the bed, stretched out the creamy white legs, and the moist opening now occupied by his fingers I was ready to jump in.

There was really one way, which made him laugh with excitement. With a messy and moist feel, pulling a finger from the center of her sweet thigh, he held it in his mouth and felt a fire rising on his face as he drank juice from his tongue.

She had never seen anything so grotesque and sexy in her life at the same time. His palm was glossy with her juices, and yet he slurped on the digit as if it had been brushed with something tasty. He just went ahead and withdrew his finger off his mouth and immediately pulled off the socks

Instead, he pulled his finger out of his mouth and reached out to unbutton the pants.

She convulsed and gasped, recalling that she was initially trying to see the penis trying to rob her virgin.

"Oh, God..." She couldn't help the exclamation as his cock was pulled out of his jeans, long and heavy, impossibly hard with a purplish head that was already oozing. And that was supposed to fit inside her?! Maybe it was just because of the situation, but she felt sure it had to be bigger than any other cock she'd ever seen before.

"On your knees Emily." Part of her screamed that she should protest, that this wasn't part of what he'd paid for, but with Mr. David's dark eyes boring, she found herself falling to a kneeling position in front of him. It was surprisingly easy with her shaky legs.

"I don't want to hurt you. I'll do it well for you," he said as he ran his hands in her hair. "But you need to take advantage first as he rubs the edge of his dick on her wet pussy, otherwise I'll take you too fast and too hard."

The young beauty moaned at his words, allowing him to shove the head of his cock between her pretty pink lips. Emily looked up at him with wide blue eyes, half nervous and half sexually aroused, with the mushroom of his cock already in her mouth. Instinctively, she flicked her tongue against it, tasting the spicy pre-cum, licking the velvety smooth head as if it were a scoop of ice cream.

He smelled of salt and musk and masculine, and she had only a second to react to what was going on before her hands pushed her inexorably back, pushing more of her dick into her throat. This wasn't the first time she offered her heart, but it was certainly the first time she'd felt out of balance while doing it. Usually, oral sex made her feel both feminine and dominant. Right now, she felt feminine and exquisitely vulnerable in a way she had never experienced before.

Mr. David had a firm hold on his hands, pulling his legs up every time he pulled his mouth down on him. She caught the base of his dick to prevent herself from gagging as he fucked her pussy. Because that's exactly what he did, raping her pussy. It was rugged, intense, humiliation piled on top of humiliation...

And it made her hotter and wetter than the rainforest.

Her body was throbbing, aching, hoping that it would touch her anywhere but her head. The space between her legs felt empty without that long finger inside her, and the tops of her thighs were sticky with her juices as she rubbed them together in an attempt to ease the desperate urge. When her head swayed, her breasts rolled, firm nipples trying to brush against something. She felt desperate to express herself, but she couldn't even imagine how much more degrading she would have been to her dignity.

The spurt of thick vegetation in her mouth caught her off balance when he pulled her head down to the point where her lips touched her fingertips, and her cock pulsed against the back of her throat. She whimpered and squirmed, trying to pull out when boiling fluid rushed into her mouth and swallowed painfully. Anything else she'd never done before, but it was vomiting or coughing. His dick's head was too far back in her mouth to spit it out, rubbing the back of her throat and sliding down towards her ass.

As he actually let go of her hands, she came up sputtering, furious.

"That wasn't part of the deal!" she glared at him. "I'm done here!" he laughed. "Not if you want the money you're not," he laughed, putting one finger under his chin and tilting his head up to look directly into his eyes. The burning light in his eyes made her shake. "Besides, if you really didn't want to do this, you wouldn't still be here on your knees in front of me. You like this. You could have walked out of this room at any moment, I know you don't really need the money, but you're still here on your knees with my sperm in your belly and a wet pussy that's just aching for her first cock. Isn't it?" Red and white splotches covered her face like an fl. His flavor filled her mouth, and even though it made her slightly nauseous, it also turned her on.

Looking at her eyes, Mr. David grinned. "You can leave if you want to, Emily. No one's forcing you to stay. You can go back to your regular life, go out with some nice guy and finally let him pop your cherry after a safe number of dates. You can as well lay your beautiful ass on the bed for me to taste, as I love tasting what I will eventually dig, I need to eat your virgin pussy.

Her feminist hand called him a mischievous cunt, a dirty old pervert, and said that she was going to hit him and storm him out now. But it was her body, libido that won, she found her lying on the bed and lying down with her legs together, she stood up and dressed completely stripped and looked with half-haired eyes. She had just sucked him, but his cock had hardened again and his clothes had fallen to the floor, so his eyes did not look away from her.

His body was well-muscled, his shoulders wide, and the hair on his chest and the line down to his groin was dark with wiry hair, with only a few gray hairs sparsely scattered throughout. Sucking in a breath, she couldn't help but paint a picture of her hard, muscular body surrounding her, her hair brushing against her soft skin. Mr. Davids didn't look like the men of his own age; he was bigger, heavier, and more aggressive. They all looked like eager puppies next to him.

When he entered the bunk, his eyes shone with excitement as it widened. She didn't know it, but the expression on her face was a combination of fear and anticipation, a total change for him. Having her young, beautiful body set up for him had always been enough to arouse, but knowing that she had chosen to stay and give up her innocence to him, that she was excited by the prospect, made his blood roar.

"On your back," he said, grinning at her in a way that made her whole body tingle. It wasn't a lovely smile, it was an insensitive one. The man he said had no doubt that she was going to do exactly what he told her to do. "And spread your legs." The act of laying on her back and exposing her body to him made her feel incredibly sexy and extremely insecure. Both of which she had grown very used to experiencing in his presence here in this house. It almost seemed that those were the only emotions he wanted her to know.

"Beautiful," he muttered under his breath, and he looked up and down at her, and she blew with pleasure. If he looked at her that way, she felt beautiful. It's attractive. It's unstoppable.

Then scared out of her mind as he climbed onto the bed then hovered over her, his arms forming a cage for her upper body, his knees lying between her thighs. Even if she wanted to, she could no longer close her legs to him. As if remembering that he was more terrifying than turning her on, Mr. David pulled back so that his weight was no longer balanced on his shoulders.

Of reality, that just meant that his hands were free to touch her. Emily moaned as he slit it over her ribcage, just under her breasts. She shut her eyes as he started to slide them up, catching her breasts with his hands. The only sound in the room was ragged coughing, and rapid intake of air as he squeezed enough heaps. Arching her back, she stifled a sigh, for some reason she didn't want him to know how incredibly good she felt. As if that would give him more control over her when he had all the power in the world

Then something hot and wet covered one of her delicate breasts, and her eyes flew open. The bristles on his lip scraped against her skin as he bit at her breast, and her hands went down to hold his head to her. He nipped it, dragged it, licked it, and softly bit it down on the sensitive nub. Under him, her body moved, writhing, sensual need between legs began to grow and began to grow every time she seduced her nipples.

She called out in frustration as he pulled his mouth down, until his lips wrapped over her other breast. The abandoned one was left chilled and wet in the cool air of the hotel room, a sharp contrast to the moist heat that had previously been neglected. Emily found herself brushing her fingers through her hair, through her arms, over her chest and back, everywhere she could go. She would never have had the urge to touch a man like this; she should naturally have allowed them to touch her, to sweat over her flesh, though she remained in control.

There's no chance of that happening here. Mr. David played his senses like an organ, with all the finesse of an accomplished guitarist. She was completely out of control, a hostage to the feelings he was stirring inside her. Even when she masturbated and made herself cum on her own, she didn't feel the cacophony of feelings, the aching, throbbing need to be kissed. It's always been a kind of therapeutic practice before; definitely not a heart-pounding, breath-taking, pussy-spasming indulgence she's been feeling for the first time. The way Mr. David handled her breasts wasn't with the eagerness of a man who thought his toys might be taken away at any moment, it wasn't with the greed of a man who would play as long as he wanted, because he knew it would turn the woman beneath him into a mound of molten desire.

"Oh, God... Mr. David..." Emily cried when he squeezed her nipple again and removed it.

"Hey, Emily?" his accent was basically purged. He squeezed her breasts hard, staring at her as she arched and scribbled.

"Hold me," she replied.

"I'm feeling you.""Please... yeah... please..." She spread her legs wide, loving her pussy and, at the same time, not caring if she'd just hit the aching wetness that had become the core of her entire world.

"Tell me to touch your pussy," he said. "Please touch my pussy." His body weight moved, moving down, and then his hands left her breasts and pushed on the inside of her thighs, opening wide open so that he could look at the glistening moist lips of her pussy as they parted. Emily's face turned dark. She wanted him to touch her, not look at her. Somehow his rapt gaze on her most private body parts made this whole situation so much more real, giving her time to recollect her thoughts and noticed that the face of her best friend's father was a few inches away from the flesh of her virgin woman.

To protest, when she leaned forward, opened her mouth and pressed against her pussy, her words appeared garbled. He was beautiful because he applied all the oral skills on her and slowly took her to lick and taste her.

Usually, this was something the guys were trying to get into her panties, and she decided desperately that this time she was going to follow it through to the end. It's with Mr. David.

Burying her fingers in his dark locks, she bucked against him as he shrugged her pussy lips apart, and began a concentrated assault on her extremely sensitive inner lips, enjoying the movement towards her glowing clit. The rasp of his tongue was like a firebomb inside her body, sending her spiraling toward the point that she was in agony.

"Oh, God! Mr. David!" he went away to her utter dismay, sucking the sparkling shine of her honey out of his mouth. The expression on his face was pure masculine contraband. "Please, I'm too tight," she whispered, pushing her own palms down to touch her swelling skin, groaning as he caught her wrists and planted them on either side of her head, the long, rough length of her body coming down to the top of her. Her mind shook and she could feel the tip of her cock pressed against her virgin skin, and the pupils expanded with hope.

"Oh no," he whispered, licking her mouth so that she could enjoy herself. Everything she would never have allowed any other man to do. "You're going to be cremating all over my dick when you come, Emily, and not before." Crude words made her gasp as her body yearned for the culmination of the image he created. Yeah, yeah... She wanted him inside her while she was coming, she wanted to feel him moving, to split her open. Emily had never masturbated with anything that had invaded her body because she had always wanted to feel the moment of her hymen giving way to a man's insistent dick. And now that time has finally come upon her.

Mr. Davids pulled back, his eyes fixed on her face as he moved his hips, and she could feel him at the entry of her body. Green eyes went as wide as they could as he nudged towards her, his own dark eyes hanging on to her face when he started to push inward. The barrier to her body wasn't strong, but he could feel the tension, hear the break, see her winch as she broke through the small barrier to heaven between her thighs.

"FUCK." He would never have felt anything like that. Not only the way her body gave beneath him, or the inner rug of victory when he saw her distressed smile as her hymen split, but also the sublime tightness of her untouched tube.

He was the first to touch her in this way, the first to feel such feelings. As much as he had loved the brief moment of agony as he had penetrated into her body, he would have treasured her pleasure even more.

"Oooooooooooo!" Emily screamed underneath him, her legs parting and falling together as her young body struggled to figure out how best to deal with her new circumstances.

"Mr. David, you're so heavy! It hurts!" he said. She was so exquisitely close that she felt like she could cut off her dick with her arms.

"Shhhh, sweetheart, it's going to start feeling good," he said, caressing her body as he slowly put his cock in the heat. It was the slickest, most velvety gloves possible, and it took all of his efforts not to crash into it.

Of course, if he wanted to, he could; after all, he would have paid for the use of her innocent flesh, paid to exploit her. When he wanted to fuck her in the bed without taking care of her satisfaction that was his right, and the dominance made his cock swell even more

But she would have done this because she wanted a man. Not a man out of control who would have taken his own fun without remembering his own.

And so he kept himself still inside her as he kissed her softly, looping his arms around his neck so that he could caress her, rocking so slowly with his hands that his penis would rub against her clit

He could feel her inner muscles contracting and loosening as her virginal sheath gradually got used to its new dimensions, accepting the length and girth of her cock. As she started rocking back into him, her arms wrapped around his waist, he knew she was happy.

Clamping her thighs, he began to withdraw, deliberately and softly, before slowly sinking back into her.

Emily was at her side with all the intense feelings. Although the mild embarrassment of her pleading, the initial pain when her virginity had been taken, and the pain of her muscles contracting to allow Mr. David to penetrate her body had somewhat lessened her anticipation, the older man was well on his way to restoring her. She couldn't believe how amazing it was to have him shift inside her, to feel him so deeply in her belly that she was sure, with every soft thrust, that he was deeper In all the right places inside her more than what expectations were from her.

Her whimpers were hushed by his lips as his tongue flew into her cheek, and she kissed him again, for at least that was a familiar thing that she knew how to do.

Surprisingly, she knows how to have sex which came as a shock to her. It was instinctive, natural, as her body responded greedily to him, needing him to be harder, quicker, stronger. Suddenly, she understood all the porns that women were begging for. Her body was beginning to hurt, deep inside, where she had never had such a need before, and her throbbing cock was driving her ache higher and higher.

Moving against him, purely by instinct, Emily could feel that he was starting to loosen some of the iron self-control he had used with her. He groaned against her lips, plundering her with a kiss as his pounding hips began to move faster and harder. It was so painful that his big penis opened and hurt her, rubbing the inner wall of her body, moving very powerfully and scraping the inner wall of her body, and it was always very good Was.

He hooked his arms under her legs, pulling them up so that she was almost bent in half, and every stroke of her body pressed hard against her clit. Now every thrust went so deep inside her that she had the wild idea that she could actually feel it in her mouth.

"OH! FUCK!... OH MR. DAVIDS!!!" screamed Emily, holding by her throat, as the most powerful orgasm of her life crashed into her like a freight train. It was hot bliss, devastated ecstasy, blinding fireworks. She can feel her inside squeezing him, rippling around him with convulsions she cannot control and does not want to control. Every hard thrust had a higher and higher climb on a wave of pleasure that seemed endless.

As he bellowed out his own orgasm and hurled deep, she could actually feel him throbbing inside her, she feels the pulse of his penis through a narrow tunnel when she begins to squeeze semen from him. She was held in her arms because they were so strongly pressed. He surrounded her, inside and outside, and she had never felt so alive, so feminine.

"Jesus... Emily..." Mr. David's voice was husky as his weight came to the top of her, pulling her further into the pillow. She liked that, closing her eyes, she snuggled her face into her chest as she felt contracted around him, shuddering little post-orgasmic bliss shudders.

"That was great," she said, in a sound of absolute awe. Suddenly, she was so glad she had done what she had done. Not only did she get something valuable and meaningful for her modesty, but Mr. David had found it a lot more fun than she thought it had been several years before. Yes, he was blunt, almost mean, with some of his words, but that only turned her on more if she was honest with herself. And the actual thing... mind-blowing to say the least of all.

"Mmm..." he pushed himself out of her, catching her in his embrace before she could object. "I'm glad you thought so," he said, looking down at the young beauty in his arms with all her hair and the reddish, oily proof of her virginity between her legs and staining her shaft. "Because as soon as we get cleaned up in the shower, we're going to do it all over again"

# MY BEST FRIEND'S DAD

Christy was lying on the swing of the porch. She rocked back and forth with a brisk afternoon wind while waiting for her best friend, Alicia, to get home.

We also attended the local community college, and after long summer days like this, we usually found themselves in Alicia's air-conditioned apartment. They would dance around and sing along to the radio as they gossip and sip ice-cold sodas, but lately, things had begun to change.

Alicia met a man named Hart at the local Dairy Queen, where he was the night manager. Christy thought he was a slut. He would grab her butt when Alicia turned her back, and once he dropped her off on his way home, he would have begged her to have sex with him. Christy despised him, man.

Christy glanced at her watch; she had been waiting for almost an hour. Alicia didn't come home early. She stood up and started walking down the porch steps as she saw Alicia's brother, Greg, turn into the driveway. She walked towards the car and waited for him to get out of there.

Greg got out of his jeep and waved to Christy. He had been home earlier than usual, and he was shocked to see her standing there. Christy was the best friend of his daughter's, and she was as stunning as they were. She was about three inches taller than her daughter, her hair was blond, her eyes were shimmering green, and her body was a perfect ten. He couldn't count the number of times he'd jack-off while dreaming that she was standing in front of him, completely naked, and playing with her huge boobs. He stood with his briefcase in his hand and moved towards her. He didn't wear a bra, as usual, and her hard nipples battled against the thin fabric of her faded antique tee, which said "Impeach Nixon.""Great top," he grinned.

Christy turned startled, looked down and grinned, "Oh yeah, thank you." She chuckled, "Yeah, you don't know when Alicia's going to be in, do you?""She told me she'd be out late. It's Hart's night off, I guess, and they're going out." He stared at her quizzically. He was disappointed that Alicia didn't hang out with Christy lately, but what could he do? He noted the frustration on Christy's lips.

"Well, thank you again," she said half-heartedly.

Greg smiled, watching as she turned to walk away. "Christy, would you like to come in and have a glass of lemonade or water?" he smiled his most welcoming smile, confidently anticipating that she would approve it.

Christy turned and flashed her brilliant smile, "Sure!" Greg walked into the house, putting his briefcase down in the hallway on the way to the kitchen. Christy pursued him like a puppy dog.

As he opened the refrigerator in the kitchen, and pointed to it, "water or lemonade?""Lemonade," she replied confidently.

"Good choice," he said, pulling out the lemonade pitcher and pouring two bottles. He set them on the table and sat down in front of her.

"Congratulations to Greg," she added. He had finally gotten her to name him Greg two months ago, naming him his favorite sex toy,' Mr. Folsom's been too odd for him.

"You're welcome," he said, nodding at her and sipping his beer. It was definitely hot there. He sat there a few more minutes before he decided to engage her in a discussion. Silence made him a hard-on. "So I haven't seen you around so much recently.""Yeah, I know," she sighed and took another drink.

"Alicia and Hart have been out a lot." Greg looked at her and put his glass down.

She smiled, looking out the window. "Well, she really likes him." She glanced at Greg, "I think since she's got a boyfriend, and I don't, we really don't have too much to chat about." He was shocked at her disappointment, and even more so by the way, her eyes started to flood. She missed the best friend of hers. "Oh, he's a slut," he said suddenly.

Christy was stunned, but she could not help but stifle a joke. "Complete," she said.

"You're too smart to go out with a prick like that, I was hoping you'd have some sense in it," he smiled. "You've got to get guys like that pounding you all the time, after all." Christy blushed, "No, not really."" A lovely girl like you? "He smiled, ' Come on, stop flattering me But I'm not, "she was already blushing. She had been dating Alicia's dad since she was fourteen, and now he was calling her beautiful. Her heart raced in her throat, "You think I'm amazing.""Gorgeous," he smiled.

"How beautiful?" she asked, giggling, what was she doing?

He blushed this time, "You're the prettiest girl I know." Christy grinned and stood up. She went around the table and sat down on her chair. She wrapped her arm around her neck and gave a big affectionate kiss on her cheek. "Thank you, Greg." She smiled, "You made my day." She was about to bounce again when she felt the bulge of the pants pressed against her thighs. He was having a hard-on!

Greg had turned the color of a dark red, too shameful! He didn't expect her to sit in his lap, but she did.

"It's all right," she said softly, still sitting in his lap. "I like you as well." Greg inhales deeply, but did she like him the way he liked? "Yeah?" He could say.

"Yes, I really like you," she told Husky, emphasizing "many." She looked at him in the eye for a second before she brushed her lips against him in a sloppy kiss.

Greg started kissing her back, but then she pulled out, "This is wrong." She looked at him blankly and said, "No, it's not." She cocked her head to her side and kissed him again, "I like you, you like me, it's simple." He let her kiss him again before he brushed her hair behind her ear. "Are you sure?" she grinned and kissed him. "Sure," she said, raising her knee so that she was straddling him. Once again, she threw her arms around him, trapped in a string of moist, passionate kisses. Greg moved his arm to her neck, then to her bottom, kneading her tight ass cheeks between her palms.

He slipped his thumbs under the bottom of her shorts and ran them over the back of her undies. He left her mouth and started to kiss her lip, then down her smooth, fragrant face. He moved one hand up the back of her t-shirt and felt her warm, youthful skin. One hand went to her melon-sized breasts. His other hand soon joined, and he began to stroke her big tits. Her nipples were so hard that he was driven wild.

She pulled back from kissing him and smiled. Slowly, she took the t-shirt over her head and hurled it into the oven. She ran her hands over her boobs and tweaked her nipples, "Do you like that?" Greg smiled widely and eagerly welcomed her deliciously taut nipples. He sucked on them and swept his hot tongue over the tight orbs, crying out for pleasure from her wet lips.

"Mmm," she said. She put his hands behind his head and softened him forward. No one had ever paid so much attention to her nipples, and she felt unbelievable; she didn't want it to be over.

He kept rubbing and licking her boobs until he realized he couldn't keep out any longer. He had been waiting to see her suck his big dick for as long as he could remember. The thought was impossible to overcome once he had invaded his mind. "Hey Christy?" he moaned, drawing her near enough to give her a soft kiss. "Please suck my cock baby." She grinned at him and slipped down his tent lap to the cool Mexican tile floor. She unbuttoned the few bottom buttons of his top and unbuttoned his boots. Slowly she unzipped, leaving the bulge of a silk boxer cascade out of her dress. "Huh," she said quietly as she got forward. She put her hand on top of it, feeling the hot throbbing sensations that culminated underneath her during her make-up session. She pulled down the boxers, and his fat eight-inch cock leaped forward.

He was fully shaved, and the sleek sensation of soft skin on the skin made both of them cringes.

"ohh noo," He moaned as she moved her fingers on the shaft up and down. Every when she reached the top of his penis, pressing softly, a fat drop of precum leaked out of his mouth.

She looked up at him, and his head was thrown back. She rolled her tongue on it and gulped its entire length. Christy had his cockhead pressed against the roof of her mouth before she had dedicated all her creativity to cramming all eight inches of it down her throat. She was scared that she might not be able to because his cock was so damn fat. We were both satisfied moments later when she was able to take more of him in her lips.

Greg couldn't believe his luck; he had a dream girl offering him the best blowjob of his entire life. He could only watch her go hard on him for a few seconds before he had to throw his head back to stare at the ceiling. He had to live long enough to fuck her, and that was all that mattered to him.

A minute or two later, Greg relieved her of his dick and made her stand up. He unbuttoned her shorts and took both of them and the string off in one ardent sweep. He put his hands on her white shoulders and pulled them to his side.

Christy's vagina was shaved as well, she couldn't take it any other way, and Greg could only imagine the pure joy he would have had in her delicately moist pussy lips. He took his dick and held it against her cunt, rubbing it against her hot, swollen clit.

She moaned loudly, pushing her hips forward.

"Easy girl," he said in the middle of labored breaths. He couldn't believe that he was ready to fuck her. He dragged her tighter and let his big cockhead disappear into her snug wet pussy. He began to push up, sliding back and forth into her slick, virgin cunt.

"Oh yes," she moaned. "Come on Greg, fuck me good!" he hurled out, feeling himself slipping into her steamy folds. "Yes, oh yeah." She buckled at him, and they fucked like mad, humping and squeezing. Lust clouded their eyes, and they felt that they were losing reality in a thick foggy pleasure.

She came hard, her cunt squeezing her dick feverishly.

It's been almost too much for him. "I'm going to cum," he screamed. He got away from her while meanwhile pumped his steaming dick.

She took his cock and thrust it deep into her mouth, milking it wildly; she needed his cum. The first wave came almost unexpectedly and shot her throat faster than she could swallow. When she felt coughing, she kept pushing her hot sticky cum on her shiny breast. He grinned at her as she drained him and rubbed his juices in her pretty, tight breasts.

When Christy had finished, she stood up and kissed him. "Thank you," she whispered to him.

"Ah no, it was a joy to me," he said. He heard a bang on the car door, and he made a dash for his shoes. When Alicia came into the house with tears, we were both dressed.

"Hart lied on me all the time!" she blubbered, "I'm so happy you're here with Christy." She threw her arms around Christy and screamed.

"Let's go upstairs," Christy said quietly. She led Alicia up the steps, looking over her shoulder to Greg, who gave her a hug.

His hand was gripping Christy's string in his pocket. Sure, he was concerned about his daughter, but he knew that Christy was going to be a better listener than he could ever hope to be. In addition, Alicia's breakup meant one good thing: he'd be able to see Christy ' a lot' more from now on.

# NIGHT LOVER BUT DAUGHTER FATHER BY NOON

When I met my wife that was it for me, she was the only woman I would need. We fell in love and stayed in love. We got married and then had kids. Well, actually, we got pregnant and then we got married. Our daughter, Kendall, was born about 7 months after the wedding. The wedding was nothing special except that to us it was the most special event ever. It was small just family and some friends. We had a great life together for over 18 years...

One night, on her way home from work, she was killed in a car accident. It was no one's fault really; just a crazy accident caused by snow and ice. It devastated all of us. She was a very well-liked and popular person. I never met anyone that didn't like her. She was 5'2 and never weighed more than a 120lbs, she had short brown hair that she always dyed but not outrageously. She had big sexy breasts for a woman her size. C cup I believe.

Our sex life was incredible and very open...more on that later but this story is about how something awesome and unexpected happened with my lovely at the time 18-year-old daughter. Kendall looked a lot like her mother, Michelle, except she is a little bit taller and smaller of the frame. She is 5'5 and very skinny with 32b breasts (I know because I do the laundry now) whereas Michelle was shorter and stockier. I, by the way, am 6'1 225 and still pretty fit for my age of 40.

Well anyway about two years ago Michelle, my wife, passed away in an unexpected car crash. I would have lost it completely but I had to stay together for my children. We were all a wreck, constantly seeking each other's company for comfort. The first couple days even weeks were all a blur...but at some point Kendall started coming into my bed at night. There was nothing sexual about it, yet, but just to comfort each other. Most nights we would cry each other to sleep in each other's arms. Many mornings I did wake up with morning wood but luckily she never noticed or said anything. It was nice having her share my bed on those nights, those nights turned into every night within a few months.

I had never thought about my daughter in a sexual way. Sure I had noticed that as she got older and turned 18 and her body started filling out that she was pretty attractive. Sure I noticed that almost every guy around her checked her out in some way. And sure I noticed that she looked more and more like her mother as the years passed by. Sure I had felt her tight little ass against me and even noticed her firm little, perky tits as they pressed against me as we slept. But I had never looked at or thought about her in an inappropriate way...Until that one night 4 months after Michelle passed away.

It was a night just like any other; Kendall was sleeping in my bed every night now. Not even starting in her bed anymore. In fact, on this night she was in bed before me already asleep. Only half of her body was covered by the blanket she had already kicked most of it off. She always did that. I noticed that she was wearing her usual pajama's a tight form-fitting tank top and loose-fitting pajama bottoms that on this night had ridden up so that her right ass cheek was visible revealing her tight ass with blue silk bikini style panties on. I crawled into bed next to her on my side facing her. When I did she roused and moved close to me her back against me, I put my arm over her and squeezed her hug like. She quickly fell back asleep and I soon followed. Many hours later I had an incredible dream about my late wife.

It was a beautiful dream, the first time I had had this kind of dream. It was a sex dream. I had had many other dreams about her but none like this. In fact, for most of the 4 months since her death, I had pretty much no sexual desire at all. I had only masturbated a few times but that was mostly out of necessity and over rather quickly. But this dream was like the real thing. I remember in the dream, she was dressed in her favorite red negligee and I was on the bed watching her walk towards me. As she got to the bed she started to rub my legs making my cock get hard.

The dream was so real that it felt real...My cock was throbbing in the dream but felt so real. I felt like a young man getting his first action. I eagerly reached for a boob. It was wonderful and felt so soft and fleshy. I caressed it and then the other very quickly. The next part of the dream I remember is her on top of me fucking me fast and furiously my hands moving from one breast to another tweaking her nipples. I came rather quickly and the dream was over.

But then it wasn't over and in the dream, Michelle was laying next to me. I could feel my still, hard cock pressing into her ass right between her cheeks. She was grinding her hips and ass slowly back and around. I pushed my cock into her more also moving my hips. My pants were back on in this part of the dream as we slowly dry humped each other. My hands were slowly caressing her shoulders and side. Her skin was so soft and tender and smooth. I could feel her hand on my hip squeezing and moving it in sync with our humping.

She was quietly moaning which just made me more excited. I started moving my hand onto her stomach my middle finger found her belly button and her stomach was so tight. I didn't remember it being that tight before but since it was a dream I didn't dwell on it. As my one finger moved around her belly button my pinkie was rubbing down near her panty line barely going under. "Mm mm yes," I heard her whisper as her ass moved up and down pretty much fucking my cock through our clothes. It felt so good, even better than the first part of the dream even more real.

Not wanting to stop the humping action just yet, I moved my hand away from her panty area and slowly moved up to her breast area. Her tank top was tight so it was easier to move my hand over it rather than under it. I started fondling her breasts and they felt so good. Our hips still moving, my cock almost ready to burst; my hand squeezing her tit just the right one this time it felt firm and perky in my hand almost too perky. I moved my hand past her tit and on to the flesh of her upper chest. It was warm and flush and she was heaving her chest. Her hand was no longer on my hip but now it had my raging hard cock in it. She was squeezing and starting to stroke it. Her hand was inside my boxers, flesh on flesh. My hand was now moving under her top to feel her breast and hard nipple. Michelle's nipples were big and wide but these were smaller and stuck out further.....

HOLY SHIT!!!!!! This was no dream...This was not Michelle. This was my 18-year-old daughter. My hand was on my daughter's perky little tit. Her hand was stroking my cock. I quickly tried to think things through. I was practically asleep, maybe she was too. Maybe, maybe, maybe.....I stopped all movement and could feel my cock going soft. She turned her head and looked me in the eye and said, "Kiss me, Daddy..."

The feel of her soft tender lips was the best thing I had felt in a long, long time. We kissed softly at first, feeling each other out. Eventually, our lips parted and our tongues probed each other's mouths. My cock hardened again as she stroked it...I moved my hand down her torso until I got to her pants again. This time I barely hesitated as I pushed my hand down, I could feel her wetness way before I actually got to her lips. Her bald mound was drenched. My middle finger started to part her lips pressing down on her clit and rubbing it before pushing down between her lips.

She managed to remove my boxers somehow as she fondled and played with my cock and balls. I was rubbing up and down her incredibly wet lips. We were still kissing but more passionately now. I push my middle finger into her pussy. More like slid, it was so wet. Her whole body quivered and shook. She bit my lip and then moaned deeply and breathily. I pushed my finger in deeper and out and then back in deeper. Fucking my little baby girl with my fingers...she rolled over on her back and let me play with her. She had to cum at least twice at this point.

I stopped and pulled her shorts and panties all the way off. She pulled me closer; I was now on all fours over her, my cock inches from her pussy. I moved my hips down a little, my cock head now touching her wet lips and then I slowly started to enter her. Her chest was heaving slightly. Her chest going up and down was a beautiful sightseeing. Her nipples, hard and poking through her tank top, which she pulled off revealing her tits. My cock was now inches deep into her pussy. I pushed it in deeply and held it there for just a second before pulling it out again. I looked into her eyes to make sure this is what she wanted too...she moaned.

I pushed it in fast and deep and then out again. I fucked her hard and fast and then slow and soft and all over again. It didn't last long.... I felt her pussy tighten against my cock as she came, causing me to almost burst. I pulled out at the last second and came all over her stomach and up to her tits. I had never seen that much cum come out of me. She smiled as she took her hand and wiped some off her tits and then licked her fingers. We then cuddled and went back to sleep.

In the morning, I awoke feeling guilty and having to pee, as I got up to go to the bathroom, I looked at her naked body. I had never looked at it the way I did this morning. Her body was so tight and firm that I felt my cock twitch a little. I shook off the feeling and went to go pee. When I got back to bed, she was gone. She had got out of bed and had gone into the bathroom to shower. I went to make some breakfast. After her shower, she came out dressed and ate. She said, "I have to go to work now Daddy, I love you," she gave me a kiss on her cheek just like every other morning. She then smiled and said, "Oh yeah, and thank you. I hope you enjoyed it too." She then left for work leaving me to ponder what would happen later that night.

All I will tell you at this point is that that would not be the last time we fucked each other. In fact, two years later we still fuck quite a bit. We really never talk about it and it doesn't stop either of us from dating or anything. We spend our days just like any other dad and daughter but at night we would touch, explore, and fuck each other.

# OH MY GOSH: WHY ME?

My wife and I married at a young age and had little money while our children were growing up. While we lived in a modest, suburban area, we could not afford luxuries such as vacations and extravagancies. We felt pangs of regret each time we heard our friends discussing their camping trips and ventures to Disneyland, and vowed to try and save more money to do nice things with our family.

This is harder than it seems: both of our children had essentially grown up by the time we were able to afford a luxury vacation for the four of us. Our son, Mitchell, was 22 and about to start a graduate program. Our daughter, Gabrielle, was 19 and about to start her second year of college. We sprung the trip on them in April, asking them to each bring a friend as we traveled across the country, staying in hotels and relaxing for two weeks.

Mitchell brought his friend, Tom, whereas Gabrielle opted not to bring a friend.

The five of us piled into our SUV and started traveling west. I won't bore you with the details of our stops – we all know why you're reading this story. I can cut to the chase:

The first evening, the hotel we had reserved failed to meet our reservation obligations: we had reserved three rooms (one for my wife and me, one for Gabrielle, and one for Mitchell and Tom). As my wife and I had a King bed and Mitchell and Tom had two queens, it was decided that Gabrielle would stay in bed with Mitchell (much to their protest). The hotel promised that another room would be available the next night. We were here for four days and decided to battle through an uncomfortable evening.

We had a delicious dinner that evening, and I drank a lot of wine and tuckered out early. When I poked my head in the adjoining suite that was shared by my children and Tom, they were all lying around and watching tv. I said goodnight and went to bed.

A few hours later I woke up, shivering. I pulled the blankets over me and tried to get back to sleep when I started hearing the rhythmic thumps of a bed knocking against a wall. I froze and listened closely. I was pretty sure that I was hearing soft moans and grunts. A rage brewed inside me as I got up and pulled open the adjoining door to the kids' suite. I froze again. There, was my son Mitchell, buried in the covers with headphones in his ears, snoring as his sister, my daughter, lay spread eagle on the bed in a white lace teddy and a garter belt getting fucked by his friend.

From the doorway, I had a clear view of him slamming in and out of her as his tongue grazed her nipples. She was arching her back and opening her mouth in a silent scream as her blonde hair flailed about from the force of their joining. I stood there, shocked, appalled, disgusted and angry watching this assault on my daughter. Not to say she wasn't willing, she appeared to be enjoying herself. Finally, I got my bearings and grabbed Tom by the nape of his neck and pulled him off of my daughter. He raised his hands in a surrendered position as my daughter, embarrassed and furious, tried to cover her body from her father.

"Get up," I said.

Angry as she was, she could not argue. As I pulled her into our room, I saw her turn back and give an apologetic look to Tom. I closed the door and locked it and led her to my wife and my bed.

"Get in," I whispered. "You're sleeping between your mother and me tonight."

"Dad-" she whispered back, but I interrupted:

"No arguments. Get in bed right now."

"Can't I change?" She was still wearing her lace white teddy and garter belt. I looked down to see her shaved pubic mound fully exposed, and her hard nipples poking out over the tops of the lace. I felt a twitch in my groin. Disgusted and embarrassed with myself though I was, I didn't want her to take her time changing and sneak back into Tom if I happened to fall asleep.

"Get in the bed."

She did as she was told. My wife, Sandra, was still snoring lightly, completely oblivious of the scene. I got in bed after my daughter and pulled the blankets over both of us so that she would have to disrupt them to get out of bed. I turned toward her on my side so that the slightest movement would wake me up. She was lying on her back, breathing heavily, probably due to the frustration of being interrupted in the middle of getting fucked.

I lay there quietly, replaying the scene over and over. Had I overreacted? She's an adult, yes. But what the hell was she wearing that for? My imagination drifted to her lace getup as she lay with her legs open with Tom between. As I thought about Tom pushing himself into my daughter, I started to get an erection. I tried to push it all out of my mind, but her nipples and shaved mound kept swimming before my closed eyes. The more I tried to concentrate on something else, the more I focused on the way my daughter's tits looked in the white lace. Before long, I was rock hard. I opened my eyes and looked at her, lying peacefully, sleeping.

I slowly moved my hand and pulled the blanket down a bit. Her beautiful nipples poked out again for me to see. I inched closer to her and pressed my boxer clad cock into her hip and ground in a circular motion. I waited to see how she'd react: nothing. I ground my dick into her hip again. Nothing. At this point, I was aching. I moved my hand across her body, under the blanket and grabbed onto her right hip with my hand as I pushed into the left hip with my cock.

Still nothing. I moved my hand from her hip and slid it across her abdomen. I rubbed for a second before tracing to her pubic mound and down the slit of her entrance. It was still wet from her session with Tom. As I traced my finger down her slit, she moved and her eyes snapped open.

"Dad. What the fuck are you doing?" she whispered.

"Shh," I whispered. "Don't wake your mother."

"Dad, that's sick. Stop it."

"Shh," I whispered again. "Just let me do this for a second and I won't tell your mother what happened with Tom." I couldn't believe what I was saying, but she stopped arguing and lay back.

I traced her slit and rolled her clit between my two fingers before I felt her hand pushing me away.

"No," she whispered.

"Come on," I inched closer and closer to her until my lips were less than an inch away from her breasts. I flicked my tongue over one of her nipples as I lightly tickled her clitoris and ground my dick into her side. When she tried to push my head away from her breasts, I rolled on top of her. I forced her legs open with my knees and flattened myself so that my boxer clad cock base was pushed up against her slit. I ground into her and moved in a figure-eight motion. I heard her exhale strongly then felt her bring her hands to my chest as she tried to push me away.

"Gabrielle," I whispered, "I'm not going to do anything bad. I won't take my boxers off - I just want to rub it on you for a minute."

"Can't you just go into the bathroom and take care of yourself?"

"It'll just be for a minute, honey."

"Please," she responded. But that was all. I continued to hump on her in a grinding, circular motion until I needed a bit more stimulation. I started pulling my hips back and pushing into her. I reached up and grabbed one of her tits with my hand and squeezed. I watched her bite her lower lip, looking at me apprehensively as I leaned in and took it into my mouth, still slowly bucking away at her.

"How much longer?" she asked after a bit.

"Just a bit," I whispered into her ear. I watched my hot breath bring goosebumps across her chest as I breathed into her neck. I pressed my pelvis into her hard and felt my cock head break free of the confines of my boxers. My naked cock was now poking out of the flap of my boxers. I slid up and down her slit, making sure that the head of my cock made contact with her clitoris.

"Dad, it came out of your boxers."

"I don't think so, honey," I lied.

"Dad," she said warningly.

"It's okay," I said. "I'm not going to put it in you, I'll just rub it along the outside."

She sighed angrily but stopped protesting. I rubbed my cock head on her clit some more, back and forth and heard her breathing become more rapid. Soon, her slit became relubricated with her juices as I stimulated her clitoris. When I pulled my hips back and pressed them forward, I felt my cock head connect with a snug, wet hole. I stopped, frozen with my cock head pressed against my daughter's opening.

Her eyes widened. "No. No –no- no- no- no." she pleaded and looked into my eyes.

I left my cock head resting against her hole for what felt like three minutes, just staring into her eyes. Her blonde hair flayed against the pillows, tits poking out from under the lace, shaking her head warningly. I looked down between our legs and the force of my movement pressed the head in by just an inch. The tip of my cock head was inside my daughter's pussy. The sight was almost enough to make me come right then. I looked back into her eyes and slowly pressed into her until half of my cock was inside her.

She gasped and pushed against my chest.

I pushed more and more, very slowly until my cock was buried inside of her to the hilt and my balls were resting on her skin. I stared into her shocked and disgusted eyes for two minutes before I began to rock. I wrapped my arms behind her, cradling her ass cheeks and ground into her.

She gasped again.

It felt so good inside my daughter's cunt, I couldn't blame Tom for wanting it anymore. I slowly pulled out, before sliding home again. My daughter began to grunt softly as I slowly slid my dick in and out of her. I reached between us and grazed her clit with my fingers again and saw her mouth contort into the same silent scream I saw her grant Tom. I continued to slowly and carefully fuck my daughter for several minutes. Every few minutes, I would stop with my cock completely filling her and lay still to check that my wife was still sleeping.

At one point, as I lay still on top of her, I felt her start to slowly buck her hips underneath me. Willing myself to believe that she actually wanted this, rather than being a stimulated body response, I continued to lie still to see what she would do. She continued to push her hips forward, grinding into me. Her hard nipples rubbed against my chest when she arched her back. Again, I looked into her eyes and saw shame, mixed with concentrated lust. I bent down and licked her lips.

All of a sudden, I felt her hands on my hips. She began to push them away and then pull them back. I heard her moan as she pushed my hips back until my dick was nearly pulled out of her tight hole, then slowly she pulled me back in until she was full again. She continued to do this for several minutes, her pressure and moaning becoming quicker and more intense with each thrust. I looked over at my wife, checked that she was still sleeping, and licked my daughter's lips again. I felt her legs clamp down on my back as she brought my cock into her with more force. There was no way around it: my daughter was fucking me back.

Her head began to roll from side to side and her eyes went into the back of her head.

"Ooh, ah, ssss, ahh," she repeatedly whispered as I retook control and started pushing in and out of her again.

I plunged and plunged, feeling our slick bodies slide against each other until I felt her freeze. She bit her lower lip and squealed, holding me tight to her. I put my hands on her hips and pushed down on them as I continued to pull my cock nearly all the way out and then slide it back in. I closed my eyes and willed myself to slow down as I did not want this feeling to end. I stopped again and lied still on top of her. She whimpered and began to buck her hips at me again. I sucked on her nipple as I pressed my thumb and forefinger on both sides of her clit. I began to pinch my fingers together, squeezing her clit.

Suddenly, I felt her pussy contracting on my cock, milking my cock for all I could give. I looked into her eyes again and saw her face filled with passion and lust, and I kissed her full on the mouth as she bucked and writhed on my impaling cock. I thought about my daughter orgasming on my cock, and I began to feel a warm tingling in my testicles.

As her orgasm subsided, my daughter seemed to catch her bearings and immediately tried to push me off of her. "Dad, please. You said you wouldn't put it in me. Please stop."

"Shh," I whispered and rammed into her hard. She gasped again as the bed frame smacked against the wall.

Fuck, I thought. In one swift motion, I turned onto my side pulling my daughter with me, and draped her right leg over my left, keeping my cock half-buried in her.

Sandra sat up and said "What is it? What happened?"

Gabrielle, who had been struggling and writhing against me, froze at the sound of her mother's voice.

"It's okay, honey. I think Gabby was having a nightmare. " I wrapped my arms around Gabrielle's back and pushed her down on my cock again. "It's okay, sweetie," I said soothingly, my cock fully filling her again.

"Poor baby," Sandra said. "Why aren't you sleeping in the other room?"

Gabrielle didn't respond. I pulled my cock out by a couple of inches and said "Honey, you know how boys are. Loud and obnoxious. She couldn't sleep so I told her she could sleep with us."

My wife turned her back on us again and said, "I'm so sorry it worked out this way, honey. You should have your own room tomorrow."

I pushed into Gabrielle again, slowly fucking her as my wife lay beside us, completely unaware.

I continued to slowly push her up and down on my cock until the deep breaths from the other side of the bed told me Sandra was sleeping again. I grabbed hold of Gabrielle's hips again and pressed down, grinding my pubic hair into her clit. I pressed my face between her breasts and licked the skin covering her sternum, all the while pushing and pulling her back and forth on my dick.

Her breathing became rapid again and I felt her hips buck independently of my force once more. Again, she was controlling her movement on my cock, rocking back and forth and arching her back. I continued to lick on her breasts while she ground herself into me, whimpering and gasping as I sucked at her tits.

I felt her fingertips touch my head and she pushed my head farther into her chest. I bit down on her fleshy mound as I felt her contract on my cock again, in the midst of her second orgasm. I felt her fingernails dig into my scalp as she grunted and I felt my own release coming on.

Once again, Gabrielle regrouped and tried to force me off of her. She could tell by the look in my eyes that I was about to cum.

"Please don't cum in me," she whispered over and over. Still lying on our sides, I grabbed onto her and fucked her as fast and hard as I could without waking my wife again.

"Dad, please don't cum in me," she said again, gasping for air at the force of my cock going in and out of her.

I had every intention of pulling out of her at one point, but feeling the breath of her gasps on my ear made me lose control. I held on to her hips as I railed into her – the warm tingling in my balls came back full force and I started to cum. I groaned and grunted as I pushed into her, imagining my sperm hitting the back of her cervix as she gasped again. I held her in my arms until our breathing returned to normal.

As I calmed down, I looked into my daughter's eyes, ashamed and embarrassed of what I had made her do. I kissed her on the lips and thanked her, as I turned away and fell asleep, not knowing what would happen the following day.

# MY CAR, MY DAUGHTER, AND I

This situation for the first time started just this passing week when driving my daughter home from cheerleading practice. It had already gotten dark by the time practice had finished and after waiting outside the school, my little girl hopped in the passenger side of the truck and kissed my cheek.

"Hey Daddy, how's it going?" I told her about my day at the office and then asked her how practice went. "Ugghhh, stupid, but only one more month, then I  will be through." Hard to believe, but she would be finishing her first year of community college and then moving away to attend the state university.

I really started to notice how attractive my daughter was becoming just a year earlier when she finished high school. Puberty had hit her pretty hard, her chest had already swollen to a D cup by the time she was 16 and the rest of her filled out and she became very curvy by the time she was 18. She had black hair, smooth skin, and bright blue eyes. She would lay outside on the back porch most Sunday afternoons in the Summer, soaking up the sun in her very small bikini.

I caught myself staring at her from the kitchen window almost every time. My mouth would begin to water and I could practically feel my body sending a concentration of blood down between my legs.

Cheerleading had helped her slim down to more modest proportions but the last time I did laundry, I noticed she was still a healthy C cup. Good genes I suppose, her mother had always been very attractive and for a man my age, I was still in great shape with broad shoulders, big arms, and peppered hair.

We lived about twenty miles from the School and a lot of times my daughter would doze off on the way home. She worked so hard at cheerleading, I'm sure it was quite difficult to stay awake after going to class for several hours followed by several more hours of intense exercise. When she said that she was tired and asked if she could lean on my shoulder, I didn't think much of it and just told her, "Sure".

She was still wearing her cheerleader outfit. She was lightly holding my hand and when she snuggled against me, I began to smell her perfume, God it was such a turn on.

It didn't help that, the way she was slouched over onto me pressed her very large breasts together, giving me a splendid view of my little girl's large breasts. I found myself instinctively getting hard.

All of a sudden, my daughter placed her hand over mine. Again, not thinking much of it, I returned the affection and took her hand into mine and we clasped our fingers together so that we were holding hands.

Things began to happen fast after that...my well-endowed daughter began to slowly move her hand against mine then moved our hands into her lap. At this point, I'm starting to sweat, I know where this is going and that I shouldn't be doing this but my daughter was SO sexy and these feeling that I had for her were so repressed...

Her eyes were still closed but she started moving my hand up her thighs to where I was just barely under her skirt. I couldn't stop. I slowly kept my hand moving up her thighs, feeling that smooth skin, noting how soft it was from the creamy lotion that she put on her legs after shaving them each day. I was surprised to discover that she had nothing on underneath her skirt, I noted as I reached her pelvic area.

It dawned on me that she had obviously been planning this. My feelings and lust got the better of me and I curiously rubbed her pussy lips with my middle finger wondering if I would get any reaction or if maybe I was crazy and she was just asleep.

My caresses caused her to stir and moan softly. I continued to rub until I found her spot.

"Mmmm Daddy" she started to breathe. Trying to focus on the road, I licked my middle finger, tasted her juices, and then pushed my middle finger inside her. "Ohh Daddy" she was breathing more heavily now. I realized that we would be home soon but that I couldn't let this end.

I finally pulled over just a few blocks from our house into one of the empty cul-de-sacs. I looked down and locked eyes with her for a split second before planting my lips onto hers. She opened my mouth with hers and we kissed like two horny teenagers for a couple of minutes. She found my dick with her free hand and started rubbing me through my jeans.

"Mmmm Daddy, is this for me?"

"Of course, it is, baby girl." I unbuttoned and unzipped my pants. I wrapped my arm around her tiny waist and pulled her on top of me. She immediately started grinding into me and rocking my truck in the process.

"Daddy, Ohhhh fuck, DADDY!" My dick began to ache and needed release. I held her waist and guided her starving pussy down onto my pole.

"Yes Daddy, I want it so BAD!" She rode me like a teenage girl driven by pure lust. I growled into her ear and spanked her ass as she continued sliding up and down my cock.

I couldn't get over how wonderful she felt, her creamy teenage pussy taking every inch of me. It was like she couldn't get enough and only cared that her pussy was being fed the dick it so lustfully desired. It didn't take long for her to cum. She climbed off me and resumed curling up next to me and at least pretending to fall asleep. My head was still spinning.

Later that night, after her mother had fallen asleep, I was in my daughter's room, pounding into her like a madman.

"God Daddy, you feel so fucking good, fuck me like this every day!"

Her mother was a very heavy sleeper, especially after a few glasses of wine. I started to get close and asked her if she was on birth control, she practically gasped, "No Daddy!"

I told her I would buy her plan B in the morning but that I HAD to cum inside of her. I simply couldn't think of anything else. My daughter perspired underneath me. Both of our bodies completely naked unashamed of our incestuous relationship. We were simply two adults fucking our brains out. My little girl's honeypot was as sweet as anything I could ever have imagined. I told her that her pussy "was made for me" and how it was going to get all of my attention every night from here on out.

She moaned "Yes, Daddy" in agreement.

I picked up my rhythm and started biting her ear lobe and kneading her exposed breasts. It got me so hot watching her tits bounce every time I thrust into her. I whispered into her ear, "You're getting Daddy so hot baby, I am going to cum in this tight wet pussy of yours."

"God, yes Daddy, it belongs to you now, please, please cum inside me, Daddy! I need it so bad Daddy, please, please cum in me!"

I gripped her ass and pulled her hair while I came inside my own daughter's 19-year-old pussy.

She continued to moan "Daddy, oh Fuck, Daddddyyyy" as I pumped my seed into her unprotected womb. We've had sex a few more times since then but my favorite is when we take little detours on the way to school in the mornings...

# TROUBLES OF A FATHER

I can't tell anyone. I want to tell everyone. I have a boyfriend!

He isn't really a boyfriend. That's why I can't tell anyone. He is older. People would kill me. Saying this is a bad situation is an understatement. I don't think he would go to jail or anything, I mean, I'm 18 and all. I graduated. I have a job. But still.

I want to tell Tanya. Tanya is my best friend. I love her. I just hate her too. She always has a boyfriend, usually a couple. Like every Friday, I was sitting there watching her get ready for a date. She tells me all about him and how beautiful his eyes are or how great his arms are. She always decides before she goes out how far it's going to go. I have to hear it all. I want to tell her how silly she is to be worried about kissing some boy or maybe letting him put his hand up his shirt. I want to tell her what Richard is going to do to me later. I can't though. Richard is her dad.

Last night, Friday, was pretty typical. I waited around for her date to show up. She likes that. She texts me for my report on what I thought, I tell her I liked his eyes or his car. It's always something stupid like that. She asked me what I thought. Tonight I said I liked his hair and pulled my T-shirt up over my head. I removed my hair and let it hang over my bare shoulders. He sat and watched me.

He is a good looking man. He is tall and muscular. He's a cop. All the numerous years we have known he shaved his head and it is smooth and tan. I like the hair on his chest and how some of it is gray. I think he is like 45 but I'm not really sure. I thought he was over 50 and said something one time and he laughed at me. He wears glasses to watch TV. His hands are so much larger than boys' hands. His legs are so much stronger than the boys I watch run around campus. I thought when we started Community College I would meet men. They were really just boys. That's what did it. That's why I seduced him.

I let my bra loose. He always closes his eyes a little when I really start to get naked. We haven't talked about it, really. I think we both know if we talked about it we would stop. I think he wants to stop. I just know that he can't.

Standing in front of the TV I pulled my shorts down. I've learned to do it slowly. I do a little turn. I bought a  striptease DVD at blockbuster on clearance. I don't really do a whole dance, just pieces of it. I turned my back to him and tugged at panties. I wanted to get sexy panties, the real ones with lace. I got embarrassed and stuck with the cute little "Pink" ones everyone wears. He doesn't seem to mind.

I think my ass is huge. I know how much bigger it is than Tanya's. My mom is the same way. We are curvy. I will get fat just like her but for now, I'm just curvy. I don't think he would like me if I were super skinny like Tanya. I think he likes that I am built like a woman. I bend my knees as I pull my panties down. It's kind of a squat move. Then, when they are at my ankles, I straighten my legs and my bare ass goes straight up into the air.

That's the end of my seduction. I go over to the couch and sit beside him. Sometimes I lay with my head in his lap. This time I stretched out with my legs up on the arm. I watch whatever he is watching, a lot of times it's Sports Center. We watch Sports Center a lot and I ask him questions. He always answers. His voice is deep and calm. After a few minutes, I rolled over halfway and took his hand and put it between my legs. I looked up at him. "Do it slowly," and I closed my eyes.

He teased the little hairs around my pussy. It was torment. I loved how it would tickle just a little. Not the squirm away tickle, it was softer and just made me melt. He would run his thick fingers over the edges of me and my legs would just creep open. I ached to feel him inside of me but that wasn't what really felt good. He just knew what he was doing. I took his finger and raised it to my mouth. I sucked it a little and licked it a lot, the same way I would suck his cock. I felt his cock twitching under my head. He was always hard. I guess he wasn't that old. I let go of his wet finger and he put it on me. Just barely inside of me. He knew where my clit was. I had read all about this in Cosmo but had never had a boy try to get to it. He did. He pressed right down on me and moved his finger in little circles. It would make my body twitch. I lied there and let it happen. I looked up at him. He was watching me but looked away. I knew he was embarrassed. I closed my eyes again so he could watch. I imagined him looking at me. I started to imagine him on top of me and they started to hit me.

I had never made myself orgasm. The way he touched me they slammed into me one after another. It was like being on a bumpy road. My body would stiffen right before they started and then shake. He said I made little squeak noises but I had no idea. When I came he would stop moving his fingers and just press his large hand flat against me.

I had a bunch of texts. They were going to a party. There would be lots of guys and beers. She told me I could get laid. I felt snarky and told her something about not fucking little boys. She said something about me dropping 20 pounds and I might be able to. She was drinking. I blew it off. She would apologize in the morning.

I wanted to blow him. I liked to lie on the couch and suck him. He didn't want me to get him off while I sucked him. I wanted desperately to. It meant that we could spend an hour lying on the couch with his cock in my mouth as I teased and licked him. I went to pull him out of his jeans and he stroked my cheek and said not tonight. I asked him if we could go to bed.

He said yes.

It had taken him months to finally give in to intercourse. I hate that word. It doesn't sound anything like what it is. It can be a lot of things. Fucking, humping, making love, but "intercourse" just doesn't say anything. For months we would play around. I would ask him and he would say no. I would climb on his lap and grind my pussy against his cock until I thought he would explode but he resisted. I got him finally. Took advantage of him actually. I felt bad the next day but I got over it.

He followed me up the stairs. I swayed my hips shifting my ass from side to side. I knew how that got him. Really, all girls need to watch that DVD! Down the hall and into his room I walked, he stayed a step or two behind me. He had three different moods in bed. I was getting good at telling which mood it would be.

That first time was what I would call angry. It's not that he is angry with me, it's just the intensity. It is true fucking. I can make it angry sex when I really want it. If we spend a weekend by the pool and he has had a couple of beers I can flirt him into it. I can make him want it so bad that he takes me. That's what I did to finally get him. Tanya and I were lying out while he did yard work. He had his shirt off and he was tan and sweaty. I just wanted him too badly to let him get away with just fingering me. I would sneak around the corner of the house and flash him my tits. I would rub myself through my bikini and he would try to look away but he couldn't.

When he finished he joined us in the pool. I went inside to get Tanya and me sodas and came out with a bottle of beer. While Tanya floated off at the other end of the pool I worked the beer bottle like a cock. He had three or four before Tanya finally went out. I pretended to leave when she did, then turned the corner and snuck in the back gate. He was sitting by the pool smoking. He hid the fact that he smoked. I stripped out of my clothes and suit and walked into the house and up to his room. He walked in behind me with a look on his face I had never seen before.

He took me hard then rolled me over. He took me from behind. It was crazy. He kissed me like he had never kissed me before. When he finished we just collapsed on his bed and laid there under the fan forever. I knew that face now. Talking dirty I could make him have that face. Sometimes I would call the house and ask for Tanya when I knew she wasn't there. He would listen and I would tell him how bad I needed him to fuck me. I thought about him being stuck at home with that look on his face wanting me.

I will admit. Friday I was mad at Tanya and was in an angry sex kind of mood but It was obvious he is feeling awkward. It could still go either way. I would find out when we got into the room.

Sad wasn't my favorite. I knew it would be sad if, when he walked in, he took me in his arms and then kissed me on the forehead. I read a lot about sex. I would find books and read stories on the internet. When it was sad I think you would call him submissive. I could do what I wanted to him. I had read about doms and subs. I hoped someday he would teach me. I read about being dominated and hoped someday he would tie me to the bed and make me a "slut." This wasn't like that.

I would kiss him and he would just lie back in the bed. I would get on top of him and ride him long and slowly. He would press his eyes closed as long as he could. He couldn't resist looking at me though. I would lean back and just let him. I could put on a little show. I would press my tits together and he would watch me cum. Sometimes, I would be there for an hour before he would finally come for me.

I was worried and sad that it would be the last time. I didn't know what he was thinking so I could only guess. I would lie in bed with him after and let him hold me. Sometimes, he would fall asleep with me in his arms and I would lie there and fantasize about every night being like this. Usually, though, before he would doze, he would get out of bed. He would tell me I had to go. He would kiss my forehead again and I would have to go home wondering if it was over.

I didn't always go home. Long before there was anything with Richard, I would stay at Tanya's house for days at a time. Before Tanya's mom left, she was more of a mom to me than my mother. A family secret, my mother is addicted to pain killers and vodka. She has always been. I don't think I will ever drink. Tanya steals Richard's beer and he knows. He asked me once if I did. I told him no and he knew better than to wonder why not. I think it's important that he knows I'm not drunk when we go to bed, I'm just guessing.

So yeah, I don't always go home but if it is sad, I usually do. Sometimes, I will sleep in Tanya's room. She will come home from a date and find me sleeping in her bed. She will crawl in next to me and tell me about her date. I will smile to myself.

When Tanya's mom left it was hard on her. It was just before her senior year. Her mom had been having an affair, for years. She betrayed Richard and Tanya. They had a love for her that I didn't have. I think I was angrier than they were. I stayed here more often after that. I would tell Tanya that her father was like my father and she was like my sister. I never thought that though. I liked Richard different than that. I don't think he knew.

Back to last night, I get distracted. I stepped into his room and he took me in his arms. It wasn't sad, it was sweet. I liked sweets. Sweets made me feel things. I know I am just a silly young girl but when he took me in his arms and looked down at me with his light gray eyes I gave myself to him fully. He kissed me deeply our bodies pressed together. I loved the warmth of him, the size of him. I felt safe like I had never felt before. He would kiss me for a long time. He would pick me up and carry me to the bed. I'm not some little thing, a boy couldn't do that.

His mouth moved down my body. I held his head against me when I liked where his lips and tongue were. I stroked his bald head as he sucked at my tits and warmed me up. He kissed my belly. I felt the same tickle at my lips and then his tongue on me.

Tanya once told me about the boy that wanted to lick her. I giggled.

I relaxed totally and his tongue and lips, his fingers and thumb moved around me, moved inside of me. He had total control. He would get me so close I could feel it starting and then he would change it up. He could make me grunt uncontrollably. I think it was a game to him. He put his finger inside of me and then took my little clit into his mouth. He pressed his tongue against me and held me against his teeth and then I knew it was coming. His finger moved. He didn't fuck me with his finger; he just moved it inside of me. I came so hard. My legs tensed to tight they ached. I gripped at the sheets and he kept going. I wanted him to stop but, fuck; I didn't want him to stop.

He let me calm down and catch my breath. He occupied himself with my body. In my mind, I called this making love. He touched and caressed me everywhere. He would lick and touch me. He would nibble at my shoulders. I laid with my arms spread and let him have me. I felt his teeth on my arms and legs. He let me recover and when I was ready for him I would simply put my hands on his back and he would move on top of me.

He entered me slowly. I felt every bit of him slide into me. I try not to say love except when I talk about his cock. I have told him I love his cock. My pussy loves his cock. My body loves his cock. He goes slow and deep. I press my hips up to meet him. I looked into his eyes and he looked back at me. He smiled at me and I kissed him. I gripped him around the neck. He was so strong I couldn't pull him down on me. He would straighten his arms and I would be pulling myself off the bed to kiss him. With our lips locked he took me. He would go faster and harder forever. It felt like forever. I wanted him in me forever.

I came differently with him inside of me. It didn't have the earth-shaking intensity he would get with his mouth. It started slowly and then just hit me again and again with each thrust. Sweet nights were different. Sweet nights he would finish inside of me. He would fill me with his hot man load. Sorry, but that's what I think of it as. I think of it as a big fat ball of gooey him. I love to feel it inside me; I love to feel him sliding inside of my wet pussy smearing his load in me. I know this is totally dirty but I just fucking love it... deal.

Sweet nights are different. We will do it again. Maybe I will be on top. Maybe he will be on top again. We don't really think about it. If I am lucky he will do me doggie style. Not the first time. The first time I want him on top, maybe the second though.

If it's hot, I can talk him into a swim. We sneak naked out to the pool and skinny dip in the dark. There is always lots of kissing.

Sweet nights I almost always stay. When he is finally done, I slip out of bed and lock the door. I climb back in beside him. I fall to sleep first. He tells me I snore. Tanya has to knock on the door when she gets home to let him know. She will text me something disgusting and I have to make sure my phone is on vibrate.

On sweet nights I want to tell him I love him. When he is asleep I do. He's even told me it back, but he was asleep.

You don't have to tell me I'm just a little girl being taken advantage of. You don't have to tell me I'm emotionally vulnerable from a broken home. You are not in place to talk about the problems I have with my daddy moreover I know all that.

Tanya is too lazy for school. She fucked around the senior year. I hate to think that if she didn't we would be off at State already. My dirty little secret, I could be there on scholarship already. I'm a brain. Haven't gotten a B since Junior High and that was bull shit, I had chickenpox. If Tanya gets in I'm sure I will go off with her.

I think about going off the pill and getting pregnant. Maybe it will happen on its own. That happens sometimes. I read about it.

My dad lives in California. I could run off and go to school a thousand miles away and put all this behind me.

I don't want to think about it. It's easier to just roll him over and fuck him again. I can take his cock in my mouth and suck him awake.

# MY LOVER'S DAD

In a recent email exchange with my lover, I remembered a fantasy I had about my high school boyfriend's dad, Mike. I started to write it all out in our emails, and before long I was masturbating to it, confessing all kinds of dirty things. Although the story below is fictional, the fantasy was very real to me when I was 18 years old. There were so many moments on Mike's back porch when I used to wish for this to happen. I've included a few sentences of my email exchange, and then the fantasy below. I hope you enjoy it as much as I did!

***

I've had another orgasm imagining all of this and I felt sort of guilty about it, so I thought I'd unburden myself here. Something tells me you won't judge me too harshly. :) I feel like such a bad girl...

You are a bad girl, and you have me smiling big.

***

I am... a very bad girl... I can hear him saying that to me in my ear, in that deep husky voice.

I'm wearing Jeff's white button-down shirt, a little drunk from being out earlier that night. The top few buttons are undone so that you can see the round fullness of my tits and the depth of my cleavage every time I lean down. The bottom of the shirt hangs to the middle of my thighs, just barely covering my ass as long as I don't bend over. And I have my panties on too, always the same black cotton string bikini ones I wore in high school. No pants, bare feet, my long brown hair in a tousled ponytail, a little damp at the nape of my neck from sweat. Of course, I've just been fucked. Jeff's still in bed watching the movie we'd popped into the VCR. I always do this, come down for a cigarette after we fuck, and if there's a bottle of wine open in the kitchen, I pour myself a glass. Jeff has the coolest parents. They never seem to care about that kind of stuff.

As I file down the last few stairs that lead into the living room, I glance at the sliding glass door to the back porch. Mike's sitting there at the patio table with his back to me, cigarette in hand, a glass of red wine on the table. I can't help but smile when I notice that Katherine is nowhere to be found. I love it when it's just him and me. I pour myself a generous glass of wine before slipping outback, startling Mike a bit, but he smiles when he sees that it's just me. "Mind if I join you?" I ask a bit breathlessly, already pulling out the seat next to him and making myself at home.

"Of course not, Joanna," he smiles and slides his pack of Marlboros across the table towards me, his eyes darting up and down my body almost too quickly for me to notice. Almost.

"Thanks," I chime a little too cheerfully, pulling a cigarette from the box. I look around for a lighter but he has it in his hand already, flicking it for me. I lean in towards him, inhaling deeply, trying to keep my eyes on his. I think of all those old movies where the sexy, confident man lights a woman's cigarette and they hold gazes just like I'm doing with Mike right now.

"So," I exhale and tap my cigarette onto the rim of the ashtray. "What were you thinking about all by yourself out here?" Mike smiles in his sexy way and I feel my pussy swelling a bit, moistening again in my panties.

"Oh nothing interesting... just work stuff," he replies, blowing a thin stream of smoke out into the night. I can't help but smile, admiring how the smoke curls from his lips like a whisper. "How about you," he grins. "Are you having a good night?"

I try not to smile too obviously. Mike knows what we do in Jeff's room before I come downstairs for this smoke. In fact, sometimes he's in his bedroom next door to us while we're doing it. Sometimes I wonder if he can hear, and what he can hear. Can he decipher my little whimpers, my moans when Jeff fucks me deep and rough? Does he hear the sound of Jeff spanking my ass, telling me what a bad little slut I am, while he fingers my hot pussy? Does he ever wonder what it would feel like, my little teenage cunt wrapped around his cock, this man old enough to be my father who I flirt with at every opportunity?

"Oh, I always have a good night when I come over to your house," I say with a smile, unable to look him directly in the eyes as I think of all the things his son has done to me tonight. I take a sip from my wine and stretch my legs under the table, flinching slightly when I feel Mike's leg brush against my bare thigh. I look up at him and bite my lower lip. I know he felt it too.

"Well," his voice shakes a little but his gaze is steady, first locked on my eyes and then traveling lower, to my mouth, watching me wrap my full lips around the cigarette and suck on it slowly, "it always sounds like the two of you are having fun." He laughs a little nervously. "Not that I eavesdrop or anything..."

"Of course you don't." I look up at him and smile, stretching again but this time letting my leg sweep along his more slowly, more deliberately, my barefoot resting along his ankle. He looks at me curiously but says nothing. "I'm sure it wouldn't be that interesting to you anyway," I giggle.

"Oh, I wouldn't say that, Joanna," he replies, his voice lowering a bit, the expression on his face a little more severe than usual. "Sometimes I'm very surprised by what I hear." I can feel the blush spread across my cheeks as he says this like I've been found out like I'm getting in trouble. I open my mouth to say something to lighten the mood but nothing comes out. I can't even look at him.

When I bring my cigarette to my lips we both realize that my hand is shaking, the cigarette quivering in the air. I hear him chuckle softly and I finally bring myself look at him. His eyes are fixed on my trembling hand. "Nervous?" he asks, with an amused smile.

"I..." my voice trails, growing hoarse all of a sudden. I smile shyly, a bit embarrassed at how young I must seem... or, maybe embarrassed at how young I am. "I guess so," I manage to say. God, he must think I'm such a baby! In my fantasies I'm never like this, so young and bashful, ashamed of myself even. I feel his hand resting warmly on the top of my knee, squeezing lightly. I gasp a bit and look up at him hopefully. He smiles.

"Do I make you nervous?"

I nod slowly, looking down but finding the courage to slip my hand on top of his where it rests on my knee. I want to keep him there, and I want so much more if I could only tell him...

He slides our hands just a little bit higher up my leg, to my thigh. My heart starts to pound in my ears, and I can feel it in my pussy. It's like my pussy is on fire, overheating, his hand so close... He's leaning in now, so close to me, whispering in my ear, "Tell me, Joanna... Why do I make you nervous?"

He pulls back to look at me as I struggle for the words to tell him. I take a deep breath. "Because... you make me feel things..." my voice is shaking. "...that I'm not supposed to feel." My cigarette rolls out of my fingers into the ashtray, like I'm too weak to hold onto it anymore. My other hand is stroking the back of his now as it moves higher, and I guide him to the edge of my panties and then further, his fingertips grazing the wet spot at my pussy. My eyes meet his and I press his fingers against the wet cotton. "Do you feel that?" I ask softly like it's a secret.

He smiles, then strokes my pussy through the underwear, bending in close to me to make it harder to stroke me. I giggle quietly. "You make me feel like such a bad girl...""You're a really bad girl, Joanna," he tells me in my ear, sternly. There, I feel his mustache tickling me, and his breath so warm. I pass my fingertips over his and allow him to rub my hot pussy through the underwear, almost like I'm masturbating with his hand...

I'm getting his teeth at my neck, his tongue now and I'm groaning. So selfish for him, I can't even control myself anymore. I slip from my chair down on the floor to my knees, kneeling in between his legs.

"I am," I muttered into his ear. I gently kiss his earlobe and then nip my teeth at it. He squeezed my pussy through the panties harder and I moaned into his ear, unable to resist yet another filthy whispering plea. "Oh, Mike... forgive me..." I step in to kiss him and he tightly holds my arms, holding me in place so I can't get closer to him inches. The look in his eyes— what does that mean? Wrath? Fancy? Apology? God, please don't let it be this...

"Would you like to be whipped, little girl?" his accent is high but still. My heart is pounding as when I was little and getting into trouble, but also from desire, my nipples pressing against Jeff's shirt, my pussy overheating, sweat flooding the core of my panties. I nod my head weakly, and he takes my hair by my ponytail, dragging my face against his jeans ' crotch. I sense his hard dick straining through the cotton, rubbing my cheek, my lip, my chin.

"Unzip my trousers and suck my cock, little slut... When you pull me all the way into your ass, maybe I'm going to reward you with a nice hard spanking..." I can't help but whimper as he asks... I think he heard us now, he felt the rough slaps of his son against my ass's tight flesh as I rub my moist cunt against his chest, bent over his lap like a dirty little girl. Will he know when Jeff spanks me, that I imagine him? Will he know that I want him to be his sad little teen slut, his cheap fucktoy? I wish he knew.... I want him to learn it all, to do everything about me....

My fingertips tremble, but I can unpull him, drop his trousers to his knees, take his hard cock out of his boxers. It's fine, long, dense and so rough, Oh god. I love how hard and so bloated it feels in my hand... I gently kiss it, indulging in the smoothness of his mouth, the taste of its precum as it spills on my tongue. Hungry I look at him and start wetting his cock with my tongue, sucking his shaft, admiring how it shines, kissing it almost lovingly, worshipfully, urgently. I want him to be good...... A cute little girl...

I wrap my lips around the tip of his cock and slowly slide my mouth inch by inch over him. I want it to feel like he is opening my mouth with his cock, like a warm virgin pussy fucking him. He groans as my lips move along his thickness, gradually. I angle my mouth so that I can keep going so that I can carry him deep into my throat, and when I do, I hold his cock there, my throat fluttering around my tip. He beams, his eyes full of desire and his palms on the back of my head, drawing me closer so that my nose pushes into his belly. My pupils are well up and I'm gagging... But it does feel so good. Can he feel how hot it makes me feel? I would just like to take more... I want him to rape my little mouth, to stuff that cock in me...

He finally releases his grip on me and I choke, gasp for air, wiping the tears out of my eyes. With his cock, he swats to my lips, so hard now and slicks out of my mouth. "Please, Mike..." I plead with him, opening my mouth as he slaps his dick between my lips. "Yes...""What a dirty little slut you are,

Joanna," he laughs at me. "Is your pussy wet?" I open my mouth to respond, but then I hesitate and slide my hand inside my panties ' waistband, pulling my fingers to expose my vagina. I gasp when I feel the creaminess of my pussy, still sore from Jeff's fucking, but unmistakably swollen and leaking now with desire... I put my wet fingertips to Mike's nose, rubbing them across his lips over and over until he traps them in his mouth and greedily sucks them on.

"Mmmm," he moans before licking and biting my tiny creamy digits. "Such a sweet young slut..." He helps me up to my feet and then gets down on his knees, his nose barely inches away from my mound. I close my eyes and just a moment later, through the fabric, I feel his breath on me, then his nose pressing against my slit, inhale... God, that feels so good on my panties, his breath so wet, his nose pressed against my clit. I whimper and rub impatiently against his chest before he finally pulls my panties down to my knees and forces his tongue into my bare pussy.

"Ohh god... yesss..." My fingertips slip into his long, gray hair and draw him back into me. My cunt ravages his lips, his mustache grinding against my smooth mound. I stuck out my legs wider for him and followed his hands back to my bottom. There he squeezes me so tightly I cough fast. He gazes up at my reaction and smiles. "Sweet little slut." Then I feel his hand stinging on my bottom, first one cheek and then another, harsher than Jeff ever did, rough and malicious. His mouth is still fixed on my vagina but his hands snap so fiercely on my ass's flesh I can't help but cry out. Squeezing my red ass cheeks, he wraps his lips around my clit and insistently sucks, shooting two fingers deep into my pussy and rubbing my g-spot while working my mouth off.

"Ahhhhhhhhhhhhhhhhhhhhhhhhhhhhhhhhhhhhhhhhhhhhhhhhhhhhhhhhhhhhhhh hhhhhhhhhhhhhhhhhhhhhhhhhhhhhhhhhhhhhhhhhhhhhhhhhhhhhhhhhhhhhhhhhhh hhhhhhhhhhhhhhhhhhhhhhhhhhhhhhhhhhhhhhhhhhhhhh...
hhhhhhhhhhhhhhhhhhhhhhhhhhhhhhhhhhhhhhhhh My body aches with it until the last surge inevitably crashes over me. He rises to his feet and unbuttons my top, pulling off his own jeans, stripping down so that for the first time I can enjoy his naked body! I'm running my fingers along his chest, smiling

over the gray hairs that I find there. Fuck that's so hot fucking... How can I want him that much even if he is in front of me right here?

I bury my face in his chest and kiss him there, my tongue running over his lips, biting softly, moving down his beautiful arms, his back, enjoying every inch of flesh to which he gives me access. My lips find his and we kissed profoundly. I can taste my cunt on his mouth and just moan. We grind inside each other, grinding his hard cock into my bare mound. God how I want that inside of me. I just want him to stab through me... As if reading my mind, he demands, "Where do you want my dick, slut?""Yes, Mike, in my cunt..." He turns me around and bends me over the counter so that my boobs are pushed against the cool glass, and my tight butt is arched towards his cock. He gently rubs the tip up and down my crack. "Wooooooooooooooooooooooooooooooooooooooooooooooooooooooooooo oooooooooooooooooooooooooooooooooooooooooooooooooooooooooooooo oooooooooooooooooooooooooooooooooooooooooooooooooooooooooooooo ooooooooooooooooooh It is torture, just long. Yet he proceeds to torment me. "Mmm, I want you to tell me something, Joanna," he says slowly, running his cock tip up and down my throat, rubbing it in my juices. "Have you ever dreamed about raping me? I mean, before tonight... have you ever... pictured it?" I turned to look at him over my shoulder and his eyes seemed to sink through me. My entire body is flushing with fear, excitement, and guilt. "I..." slows my voice as I try to take a deep breath and start over again. "I've... sometimes I'm trying to pretend it's... innocent... like, a little schoolgirl crushed...""Innocent?" he's laughing, and then he's shaking my ass. "No, I don't think it's that..." when his hand cracks down on my bottom I scream helplessly, and this time he's adamant, he's not messing about.

SLAP! "When you love Jeff, do you dream about me?" My eyes now beg as I look back at him. "Michael... don't make me answer that..." from behind he drives his cock's tip into my pussy and continues to fuck me with the edge, only one inch, and I'm beginning to groan. He is rubbing my butt over again. "Would you like more cock, Joanna?" I whimpered and nodded. "Tell me then, you filthy little slut. Tell me... Do you think of me when my son bends you over his knee? Would you like it to be me?""God, god... Yes... I think of you, Mike... I wish you were, teasing me just like you are now... I wish you filled me with your dick!" My eyes well up, and I can see my face turn red with embarrassment. I'm so hungry for this love, I'm going to say it, but he knows it's true. I can hardly look at him, but I feel my cunt leaking down my thighs obscenely...

SLAP On! "Fuck, you fucking, fucking bitch!" I groan as he spanks me harder than ever, turning my butt into bright red. "Beg me for my cock, little whore. Beg me to fuck your hot little teenager cunt!""Yes, please!! Please, Mike.... Fuck me... I beg you, bury that cock all the way inside of me... oh, please!!!""Ohhhhh!!" the cock of Mike is bigger than the one of Jeff... He fills me so full... I groan as I remember it was less than an hour before I had his son's dick in me. I sound like a little slut, the cheap... And that just makes Mike cooler. Holding my hips tightly, he pushes his dick out of me only to push it violently back in, my body jerking with every thrust forward. He pulls tight on my ponytail and pounds me harder, harder than I was ever fucked up. "Please, god, please... oohhhh yeah, I'm so close!!!" He abuses my cunt over and over again until my feet drop from the wall, my entire body stretched out over the bed.

"God, that pussy's so goddamn hot... come for me, you whore... Come all over my cock!" I scream out again and my cunt starts gripping at his hard penis, juicing all over him, dripping on his nuts... I gasp, utterly swept up in ecstasy, but he manages to pound my weak little cunt, relentless until I beg him to slow down.

This takes me a few seconds to compose myself, to feel my feet again touching the ground. He slips his dick out of my cunt and I rise to face him. My muscles are still shaky from my climax, so I draw him tight to me and kiss him hard on his neck. His mouth feels amazing against me, and I'm so hungry for more of him, sucking on his lips, wanting to get him into me, holding him in. He raises me off the ground and sits on the table's side, breaking our embrace and looking straight into my eyes. His hand travels down my naked body, across my boobs, through my flat stomach, his fingertips tracing the shape of my swollen pussy lips but then going down, backward. As I feel his fist gently rubbing against my anus, I scream and he looks at my face with a horror expression. "Jeff hasn't fucked you out there yet?" I slowly shake my head, I can't speak, my heart is starting to pound. I never even felt I was affected by it, let alone fucked there. And yet, as they rub up against my anus, I find myself rubbing against his fingertips, spreading the juices from my vagina to that very private place. He bends to my ear and says, "I haven't cum yet, Joanna. Do you know about what I'm saving it?" I shake my head slightly, but I do, of course. God, can he hear my chest pounding? My entire body tightens around him, just like the fear has exploded everywhere. Because I  cannot tell him no, but I can't imagine saying yes...

"I want to fuck you where no one else has," he says evenly, moving his lips against my ear. "Not even Jeff." When he speaks, my eyes are up and I sense a tear trickle down my face. Could he hear it? Does he any idea how terrified I am? I wish he knew... "Hey, are you going to be a good little slut and take my dick out there?" he steps back to look at me, wiping with his hand back a tear from my cheek. I kissed my head softly, nodding, licking my ear gradually, his breath warming me up. "Good girl." His mouth moves gently down my body, so soft now, almost like a different person, his tongue brushing over my rough breast, his beard tickling my navel. He's planting soft kisses along my slit, licking and wetting me again. I'm lying back at the table, pulling my legs up to my chest and revealing my virgin rear to his glare. I feel his tongue moving back too gradually like he never gets there, but he does, and then I gasp quietly as his tongue brushes along my pussy, wetting me, touching me. Without a purpose to it, I find myself drawing my legs farther back, offering him more to taste, encouraging him to enter me with his tongue in silence. "Ohhhh..." I gasp as he finally opens to me, first with his tongue and then coated in my pussy juice with his touch. "More the... Michael...."

He stands up and pulls me to the very edge of the table. I'm still bent back all the way, my pussy, and ass open to him, waiting to be violated. My eyes are on his, and I see for the first time the look of pure lust in his face as he rubs his cock along my slit and then further back, pressing against my virgin ass. Gently, he starts pushing the head inside me and I whimper, my breath catching in my throat when I cry out in pain. I feel so stretched, such an invasion, so wrong... I'm shaking my head, trying to take deep breaths, anything to accommodate this thick cock filling my most private place.

He groans. "Ohhh god you're so fucking tight, Joanna... Mmmmm...." I feel him sliding inside me slowly, every inch of his length filling me like he'll never stop... I bite down onto his shoulder when he tells me that he's buried all the way inside me now, his cock in my ass, he's saying it over and over again, holding himself inside me until I start to relax a bit. He takes my hand from behind his neck and moves it down to my pussy. "Play with yourself, Joanna..."

I slip my fingers between my pussy lips and gasp when I realize how wet I am. He smiles. "You like that, little girl?" Starting to move his cock inside me now, in and out, slowly. I can feel myself stretching to fit him, to take him into me, almost like he was meant to fuck me in this forbidden little hole. "Ohhh, god..." my fingers working faster now, something changing inside me, something unraveling, like I want... "more... Mike... More, please... I can take... harder...."

He groans and sinks his cock all the way inside me, then starts to fuck me in earnest, pumping me full of his length, pounding into my tight virgin ass, and I'm moaning, we both are now, every profanity we've ever known. My pussy is so wet I can hardly find my clit through all the cream but I do and I rub myself so hard, as hard as I've ever done it before, edging towards an orgasm unlike any I've ever known. His hand is on my throat now and he's holding me down flat against the table while he pounds me, and fuck it feels so good, his fingers wrapped around my neck, his cock buried in my little ass, my clit swelling, my pussy dripping, so close now, I hear him groan and I do too, both of us unleashing on each other. My whole body is throbbing, clenching, milking the hot cum from his balls and feeling it fill my ass, shooting so deep inside me, someplace I didn't even know existed until now.

Seconds pass, but it feels like longer. He's laying on top of me, panting, until his cock finally softens and slips out of my ass. I sigh when I feel him slide out of me, an emptiness I never felt before. He falls back into his chair and pulls me with him, peeling me off the table and drawing me into his lap. I wrap my legs around his waist, kissing him softly. "Mmm, I can feel that cum leaking into my lap, dirty girl," he says. I grin and untangle myself from his embrace, dropping to my knees again on the floor. I know what he wants... I don't even have to ask. Slowly I lick the cum from his thighs, my eyes wandering from his lap to his face, meeting his gaze. He guides my face to his cock and I open my mouth, licking him there too, eating every drop of cum as he runs his fingers through my soft hair. "That's it, little slut... Clean my cock with your mouth..."

We reassemble ourselves after a few minutes, and I look back at the sliding glass door, debating if I should go upstairs and join Jeff in bed. Mike notices the look on my face and smiles gently, offering me a seat beside him at the patio table. He opens his pack of Marlboros and offers me one. "Don't you normally do this... afterward?"

# SUPPOSED NEXT HOUSE DADDY

For Olivia, turning eighteen offered up a whole new world. It was a day she had looked forward to since middle school, and finally, today, she was able to celebrate her liberation from childhood restrictions. No more curfews, no more begging for her parents' permission if she wanted to pierce her ear, and from now on, Olivia's age wasn't a limitation when it came to men.

Olivia, as excited as she was, took her time getting ready. People would be arriving for her party around noon, and it was still only ten. It is certainly no way she will allow her eagerness to celebrate, keep her from looking as beautiful as possible. After a long shower, Olivia stepped onto the tile floor of her bathroom, wrapped in a towel. She opened the door to let out the steam and admired herself in the mirror as it began to unfog. Her blonde hair, usually the color of sand, if sand were made of silk, hung slightly darker with the wet, down past her shoulders.

The dripping locks framed her head and made her stunning blue eyes stand out even more than they usually did. The body that twelve years of dance had sculpted, small-framed, but lithe and toned, made it impossible for her not to smile at her reflection with a devious, and prideful, glint in her eyes. The fact that she was finally eighteen played over and over in her head. 'Even if I still might look sixteen,' she thought. It didn't bother her. Olivia knew it would only add to her appeal.

After drying herself off, and finishing up her morning routine, Olivia stepped into her bedroom and looked at the outfit she had picked out for herself the night before. A blue sundress, low cut, offering an inviting view from above, and hemmed just above her knees, showing off her long, shapely legs. A spiraling white floral pattern guided any observer's gaze around the young girl's toned body, over her enticing chest, with the end of the vine steering the stare up towards Olivia's eyes.

A specially chosen outfit, innocent enough to keep her dad from complaining, but provocative enough to guarantee the desired admirers at her party was sure to notice. Despite Olivia's two-year relationship with her boyfriend, Matt, teasing other men remained one of her greatest pleasures, and today, she had every intention of indulging it.

Olivia hooked her black push-up bra on the front button and climbed into her matching shorts, gazing at herself in her full-length mirror from every angle, and changing her 30 b-cup breasts so they looked like c's. Olivia slipped into her dress after she had been pleased, running her hands over the soft silk to smooth out any creases. Olivia re-entered the bathroom and applied her lipstick. With just enough eyeliner to make her deep-sea irises shine and whenever she spoke, a dark red lipstick she knew would lock men's eyes on her jaw. She looked above herself and did not even attempt to fight back her small smirk of pride. She had known that she deserved it.

Olivia scarcely touched the ground and bounced down the stairs, turning into the kitchen, kissing her dad on the cheek and sitting next to her mother.

"Happy birthday, sweetheart," said Olivia's dad tossing an apple to her. "You look absolutely beautiful.""Happy birthday, Honey," her mother said lovingly squeezing out her hand.

"Thank you guys," responded Olivia, with a warm smile. "Can I help start setting up the backyard?""Finished as you thought," Olivia's mother said laughing. "In about a half-hour people should start coming here."

...

Right on time, people started trickling and soon pouring in. Dozens of friends from school, including Matt, and all of them telling Olivia how beautiful she looked. By one o'clock the backyard was packed, and the smell of the grill filled the air. The drink in Olivia's hand, pleasantly making its way to her head, giving her face a gently blush that only added to her charm.

After spending a polite amount of time, moving from group to group with Matt, thanking everyone for coming and showing off her college-bound, football-player boyfriend, Olivia made her way back to her parents, on her own. She found them with a crowd of neighbors, her brother, flanked by beer bellies, manning the grill, and her mom seated with the other neighborhood ladies under the umbrella, covering the bar. Then sitting at the table and finishing her cocktail, laughing at the constant stream of not-so-subtle, crazy remarks from half-drunk mothers about the suddenly legal status of Olivia, despite her gentle reminders she had a husband. It didn't take long for Olivia to start looking around the party for guests with whom she hadn't yet spoken and who could save her.

Just then a cell phone began to buzz on the table. Olivia's next-door neighbor, Alexa Hoyt, picked it up and answered it.

"Hello, this is Doctor Hoyt," she spoke into it, pausing to listen. "Alright, have him prepped. Expect me at the earliest time as possible she answered, hanging up the phone and standing up. "I'm so sorry. Emergency at the hospital. I've got to go."

Olivia, along with the rest of the ladies, said goodbye and good luck, then stood up, giving her a hug, and thanking her for coming. Alexa hurried over to her husband, David, who was standing with all the other dads by the grill. She let him know that she had to leave, gave him a kiss and rushed out of the yard's side gate.

Olivia didn't watch her leave. Her eyes were still on David. He had moved in next to them, along with his wife and daughter, about ten years earlier. She'd had a crush on him for the same amount of time. Since then, it seemed like he'd only gotten better looking. His dark hair had formed faint, enticing grey flecks, his subtly tanned and softly weathered skin, as shown by his body's muscular contours as it was the day they landed. Olivia looked long enough to notice Him. He tilted his head for a moment to meet her eyes before they both grinned slightly and looked away.

Olivia looked down at her empty drink and decided it was time to head inside for a refill. She stood up from the table and made her way through the sliding glass door, closing it behind her. After ladling a generous amount of the heavily tequila-ed punch into her glass, Olivia took several swallows, then leaned back, eyes closed, against the cold stainless steel of the fridge to cool off.

Olivia heard the sliding door open and lifted her eyelids, again meeting David's gaze as he walked into the house, empty beer bottle in hand.

"Hey birthday girl," he said warmly, giving her a teasing smile. "Toasty out there."

Olivia returned his smile, and answered, "Hey, Mr. Hoyt! Yeah, it's a little warm... had to step inside for a sec. Did you want another beer?"

"Yeah actually, that'd be great, thanks!" he said, still smiling

Olivia opened up the fridge and grabbed a beer, popping the top off on the opener bolted to the fridge door. "Here ya go!" she smiled. Searching for something to talk about, Olivia's mind went to David's twenty-two-year-old daughter. She asked, "How's Dana doing? I feel like I haven't talked to her in forever," leaning back onto the fridge.

"Oh, she's fine. Just finishing up her senior year, got a job lined up already," David said proudly. "I remember not so long ago when she'd come over here to babysit you. Not long after that, I remember when you'd come over to our house so the two of you could watch scary movies in the basement."

"That was so great! We were basically sisters," Olivia laughed.

"So, your dad says your off on a dance scholarship next year. That's fantastic! You know it's crazy to think that after ten years of living next to you, I have not seen you dance once; barring the backyard displays," he teased.

Olivia, approaching the bottom of her recently filled drink, laughed pleasantly embarrassed. "You weren't really supposed to see those. Actually, my parents put like a compilation of my most recent shows on the T.V., if you wanted to see..."

"I'd love to!" David said brightly, taking a sip. "Lead the way!"

The two of them stepped over into the empty living room, where the video Olivia's dad had made was playing on repeat. She had driven through the most skimpily clad appearance by Olivia in halfway. Her name escaped her, but Olivia was wearing a dark upper linen cover that showed as much as an invitation to a contrasting skirt that soared every time she turned. At the sight of it, Olivia turned bright red and looked down at her the last of her drink, quickly finishing it.

It wasn't until she saw David's reaction, that Olivia forgot her embarrassment. Failing in his effort to appear unaffected, his breathing had picked up, and he had begun to blush. Olivia glanced down quickly and saw that the outline of a bulge had begun to grow in the left leg of David's khakis. David had noticed his reaction too and quickly looked for a place to sit down.

"Wow!" David said, forcing the return of his relaxed tone. "No wonder you were offered a scholarship! I thought you walked gracefully, but this is a whole 'nother level."

"Thank you so much!" Olivia bubbled in her most innocent tone. In a seat across from David, Olivia sat down, crossing her legs, so that the hem of her dress slid up. "You're so sweet to say that," a smile tugging at her lips.

David, looking down at the bare thighs of Olivia, then to her hypnotic gaze, struggling for a fatherly grin, then for a deep swig of alcohol, turning his eyes back to the T.V.

"I'm gonna refill my drink. Can I get you another beer?" Olivia offered.

David laughed lightly, "It's not like I'm driving home, right? I'd love one, thanks!"

Olivia stood up, providing David with an effortless sway of her hips as she passed him. She had no doubt he was watching her as she walked back to the kitchen. Now out of eye-shot of the older man, Olivia let her excitement show on her face but stifled her squeal. She could feel herself getting wet at the thought of turning-on her married neighbor, a man she'd had a crush on for as long as she'd known him. Her heart pounding and the smile on her face growing, Olivia took several deep breathes as she opened up the fridge, pulling out two new beers. She opened them up and walked back into the living room.

"Here ya go!" Olivia said offering one beer while taking a sip of the other. "It's too bad Mrs. Hoyt had to leave so early," she said casually and taking the seat next to David.

"Yeah, just part of the job," David answered, seeming to have calmed down, and smiling back at Olivia.

"Any idea how long she'll be?" Olivia posed lightly.

"Probably going to be a late night. Seemed like it was bad," he answered leaning back and taking a sip.

"Hmm, guess you've got a bachelor pad for the night, huh Mr. Hoyt," Olivia teased.

David laughed and said, "You know, you're eighteen now. You can call me by my first name."

Olivia laughed with him and replied, "I don't know... it's a habit, why break it? Right, Mr. Hoyt?" following her words with a slight lean forward, an alluring smile, and a brush of her hand over David's leg, lasting just a moment.

David, eyes involuntarily flashing down at the valley created by his teenage neighbor's breasts, then quickly back up into her piercing, sapphire stare, he felt the bulge he'd fought off, returning with force.

"Whatever you say, Olivia," David answered with a light laugh. "Maybe we should get you back to your party."

Olivia laughed and said back, "Yeah I've probably neglected the rest of my guests long enough. It's just hard, you know? Playing hostess, I mean..." Emphasizing the word she knew would excite him the most.

The married man and his teenage neighbor walked back out to the patio, shared one last smile, and separated. David went back to the dads gathered around the grill, and Olivia, the subtle, proud, smirk she'd worn several times that day, back on her face, walked over to her boyfriend, letting him put his arm around her. Unable to even feign interest in the conversation her friends were having, Olivia's mind was still fixated on the man standing next to her father.

...

The rest of the party went by slowly, people gradually beginning to leave after saying goodbye to the birthday girl. Olivia's large group of friends, boiling down to just a few people, Matt among them.

Matt leaned down, his arm around Olivia, and whispered in her ear, "Hey babe, did you feel like heading up to your room for a little?"

Olivia looked up at him with an apologetic pout on her face, and a hand on his chest, she answered, "I'm sorry, baby. I'm way too tired right now. I promised I'll make it up to you though," smiling and kissing him quickly on the lips.

Matt smiled down at her, "Don't worry about it. I think some of us are gonna head over to Duke's house to hang out for a little. Did you feel up to coming?"

"Nah, not tonight. You should go though! Have fun, Mattie," she said, giving him another quick peck with her lips, the boy having no idea how insincere her kiss really was. Even as Olivia gave it to him, her mind was filled only with thoughts of another man.

It was getting dark as Olivia walked the last of her friends out to say goodbye. She hugged each of them, and kissed her boyfriend one more time, before closing the door and hurrying up the stairs to her room. She got undressed and jumped into the shower, this one far less leisurely than the one she'd taken that morning. After getting out, Olivia retraced the beautifying steps she'd taken ten hours earlier, except this time she didn't put on a sundress. This time she pulled out the matching set of pink lace lingerie that Matt had gotten her for their anniversary. After putting them on, she pulled a white T-shirt over her head, tying the front into a knot, and then stepping into a tantalizingly short, red plaid skirt. Walking back into the bathroom, Olivia reapplied her makeup, using a little more eyeliner than before, then coating her lips with the shade of red that matched her skirt.

She stepped back and looked herself over, taking deep breaths to calm herself down. Her hair was perfectly messy, her knotted top showed off just enough of her toned stomach, and her pink lingerie just barely stood out from behind the white fabric of her shirt. Pleased with herself, Olivia slid long white socks up to her calves, and then, finally, a pair of black, low-top Converse sneakers. Olivia listened for a second at the top of the stairs, to make sure her parents were in the other room. Certain that they were, the eighteen-year-old ran down to the first floor, then out the front door, yelling as she went,

"Hey, I'm gonna meet Matt and some friends over at Duke's! Thanks for everything today guys! Be back later!"

She heard the rushed response as the door closed behind her, "Have fun! Stay safe!"

Olivia jumped in her car and starting it, pulling out and driving just around the block, parking on the street. After making sure she was out of sight of her parents' house, she started walking back the way she came but turned into the driveway right before her's. Taking a few more deep breathes, Olivia calmed herself down, then raised a hand to knock on the house's side door. After ten long seconds, David opened it.

"Olivia," he said breathlessly at the sight of her in her carefully selected outfit, that turned the already stunning young girl, into something nobody could resist. "What are you doing here?"

Hands behind her back, causing her chest to be pushed out, Olivia, swaying, chin down, eyes up, greeted her older neighbor, "Hey Mr. Hoyt... I was just thinking; we really didn't really get a chance to talk as much as I would have liked... I figured maybe we could fix that," then giggling, the light from inside catching her sparkling blue eyes, "Plus I got you two drinks today... I thought you might want to return the favor..."

"Jesus Christ," David almost moaned under his breath, then shaking his head, "No. No, Olivia, please. Alexa could be home any minute. I can't let you in. You know that."

Putting a hand on David's belt and gently pushing in, Olivia said in a quiet voice, "She's not gonna be home for a long, long time... Let's just have a quick drink, and finish talking... I promise, Mr. Hoyt, that's it,". By her last few words, David had opened the door enough for Olivia to walk in. Her hand still wrapped around the belt, her eyes filled with lust, the teenage girl, with almost no space between her and her much older neighbor, stopped her face inches from his, her glistening red lips, only just parted.

It was only as she started to see David's head begin to lower to hers, that Olivia broke off her alluring stare. She turned and began to walk down the hallway towards the cavernous living room, looking over her shoulder and in a hushed, flirtatious tone said, "C'mon, Mr. Hoyt. Let's have that drink..."

Without breaking stride Olivia used one foot to pull the shoe off the other, leaving them lying in the middle of the hallway forgotten. David, standing in the door, mesmerized at the sight of Olivia's smooth and toned legs, carried her tight, athletic body away from him, swaying the whole time. Feeling almost drunk, although it had been hours since he'd had a sip, he followed the teenage girl further into his house.

Olivia, bouncing lightly across the floor, moved to the little bar, hidden inside an old-fashioned globe in the corner of the living room. In a bubbly voice that forced a little smile from David, Olivia called back to him, "Does whiskey sound good?" As she lifted up two glasses with one hand and a crystal decanter with the other

"Yeah," David said hoarsely, then clearing his throat, "Yeah, I could use one. Just one though..."

Olivia smiled over at the older man sitting down on his couch, looking dazed. She poured each of them a generous amount of whiskey, then using the graceful, subtly seductive walk she'd earned over her years of dancing, she moved back towards David. She handed him the glass of dark liquid, then sat down next to him on the couch, so close that her thigh touched his.

Raising her glass with her stunning smile, she jokingly said, "Happy birthday, Olivia..."

Touching his glass to the young girl's, David responded with a quiet, "Yeah, of course! Happy birthday... Olivia," then followed it with a heavy swallow from his deep glass. Neither spoke for a minute. Olivia, taking occasional sips, stared smiling at David. David could only look down at his quickly depleting glass. "Olivia," he started in a low voice, "what are you doing here?"

Putting her free hand on David's thigh, Olivia dared softly, "Tell me to leave..." David didn't say anything back, so Olivia took the hand she hand she had on him, and started to gently massage his leg.

David finished the rest of his drink, his deep breaths betraying his nerves, said, "Olivia, we can't do this. I'm married. I love my wife. You even have a boyfriend."

Whispering in the same soft voice, the young girl responded, "neither of them is here right now... It's just you and me, Mr. Hoyt."

Still not looking at her, David shook his head lightly and said, "This is wrong. You're friends with my daughter. I've known you since you were eight!"

Keeping her calm, seductive hushed tone, and still running her hand over David's leg, Olivia answered, "I'm not eight anymore, Mr. Hoyt. We both want this." At her last words, the young girl let her hand drift farther up and in, towards something that Olivia was sure would be very hard. She started to feel it farther down the leg than she had expected, and her fingers running over it were accompanied by David's surprised gasp. He grabbed the teenager's wrist but didn't move it away.

"Olivia... Please... We can't," he said, clearly fighting his desire.

Olivia pushed her captured arm forward, and David made no attempt to keep it from slipping through his hand, as the newly legal girl began gently rubbing his cock through the fabric of his pants. "We can, David. Just tonight... Don't fight it," Olivia whispered in his ear, leaning forward and lightly touching her full, young, deep red lips, to David's for the first time.

David didn't do anything for a split second, then taking his teenage neighbor, he pulled her into his arms, returning her passionate kiss with even more enthusiasm than Olivia. After a few seconds, he broke the kiss, pushing the girl straddling his lap, back from him gently by the shoulders. "Don't call me 'David'. Call me Mr. Hoyt," he instructed her, drawing a huge smile from the girl resting on his legs. The smile only lasted for a second, because David quickly brought her face back to his, kissing her deeply, and sliding his tongue into Olivia's mouth.

As David's hands began to grope at the young girl's perfect body, sliding up and down her back and squeezing her toned ass with his eager hands. Olivia moaned against the older man's mouth at his touch, running one hand through his hair, and the other over his powerful chest and arms. Encouraged by the force of his hands on her body, Olivia began to grind her ass into David's lap, causing his hard cock to strain against his pants even more than it already had been. It was his turn to moan. David buried his face into Olivia's chest and used his grip on her hips to make her grind against him even faster. His wife totally forgotten, David raised his head to the teenage girls and staring into her clear blue eyes, moan out, "I want you. Oh Christ, I fucking need you."

David stood up, causing the young girl to let out a squeal of delight and laughter. Olivia wrapped her smooth legs around the older man and allowed herself to feel wonderfully powerless in his powerful grip. Sliding both of her hands over his body, and her mouth tasting his neck, Olivia watched the pictures of David's wife and daughter go by as he carried her to the bedroom.

"I've wanted this for so long, Mr. Hoyt." Olivia breathed into David's ear. "I want you to use me the way you've always dreamed of."

With only a grunt in response, David opened the bedroom door so fast that it slammed into the wall, the doorknob leaving an imprint against the white paint. As he approached the bed he turned around and sat on the edge of the mattress, again pressing his lips against Olivia's, pulling her into him even harder. He allowed his hands to explore even further than they had before, reaching greedily up behind her, underneath her shirt and beneath the young girl's plaid skirt, drawing even deeper moans of desire from Olivia.

After a few minutes of steadily intensifying passion, Olivia leaned back from the older man, undid the knot at the front of her shirt and slid her top off of her shoulders, showing the pink lace she'd worn for the man staring at her. Running her hands down his chest and over his abs, Olivia started to slide off of David's lap to go to her knees in front of him. Before she could, David surprised her and used one rough hand to grab underneath her, and turn the young girl over, her back pressing into the bed. Before she could react, David was on top of her, one hand by her head, the other running up and down her toned belly, then squeezing her covered breast lightly. He leaned down, kissing her deeply, before slowly working his head down her body, pressing his lips against her flawless skin as he went.

Olivia didn't know what to do, so laying still, hands by her side, and staring at the ceiling, she started to breathe even heavier, her previously confident face, becoming slightly nervous. Olivia's legs hanging over the edge of the bed, David, kissing his way past the teenager's belly button, began to pull down the young girl's skirt. Olivia arched her back to allow the older man to take it off with ease, revealing here matching pink lace panties, already soaking with anticipation.

David wasn't done teasing her yet. Hearing her breathing intensify just from him moving down her body, had excited him than even seeing her at his back door had. He started to tease her through her panties, sucking gently at the top of her pussy, causing the young girl to press her head and hands harder into the mattress, and drawing light moans of ecstasy from between her soft lips. Raising his fingers to Olivia's hips, David reached underneath the bands of the lace lingerie and began to slowly pull them down, revealing the teenage girl's shaven pussy.

"Fuck. You shaved little slut," David teased, drawing a quiet giggle from Olivia as she looked down at the married man between her legs.

"You like that Mr. Hoyt?" Olivia asked innocently.

In reply David moved his mouth to gently nibble Olivia's inner thigh, then brought his tongue to the bottom of her pussy, dragging it agonizingly slowly up towards the teenager's clit. A guttural moan came from Olivia's throat as she drove her head against the mattress, eyes shut, and reaching down to put one hand on the older man's head as he licked her pussy like no one ever had.

"Oh fuck! That's so good Mr. Hoyt! Don't stop! Don't stop!" the young girl begged as the older man reached her clit.

Smiling, David started again at the bottom, repeating his journey up, dragging his experienced tongue over Olivia's young pussy. After a few short minutes, David decided to take his oral torture a step further. He stopped his mouth at Olivia's clit, and brought his mouth, in a small "O" shape to the teen girl's button. He sucked it into his mouth with mild force, and the second it was in his mouth began to circle his tongue around it.

Olivia's closed eyes opened wide and rolled hard to the back of her head. Her cry of pleasure caught in her throat for a half-second, then clawing into the bed sheets and arching her back, Olivia let out a shriek of absolute pleasure. Writhing against the bed, causing the sheets to slide from the corners, Olivia was only held in place by David's strong hands on her legs.

"Holy FUCK! YES! YES! YES! DADDY YES!" Olivia screamed out, not caring if her parents, right next door, heard her. "Oh my God, that's so fucking good! Oh my God, I'm cumming Daddy!" Feeling a warmth start in her belly, then move like streaks of lightning over every inch of her body, her hand on the back of David's head, Olivia let out an otherworldly shriek, allowing her body to shake then collapse and sink into the mattress eyes closed.

Olivia was still recovering when she heard the light sound of metal on metal as David unbuckled his belt. The teenager opened her eyes, a smile growing on her face as the man, who just pleasured her into the greatest orgasm of her life, raised his shirt over his head and slid his pants to the ground. She stared at the massive bulge pressing against his precum soaked underwear, trying to hide her nervousness at its clear size. She dragged her stunningly blue eyes up from the hardness outlined at David's groin to the older man's eyes.

David stared down at the exposed teenage girl laying in his wife's bed. No thoughts ran through his head. His mind was running on a combination of pure instinct and raw desire, for this little high school girl who had just called him 'Daddy'.

"Come here," David said in a low voice.

Her smile was naughty and excited Olivia stood up pressed against the older man, then slid down his body to her knees. Perfectly level with the massive cock straining towards her, Olivia ran her soft hands slowly up David's legs, looking up into the married man's eyes, and kissing his hardness through his underwear. Her hands finally reached the waistband, and Olivia dragged the last garment down, forcing David's tortured cock to finally spring free, pointing away from its groomed base.

Olivia gasped and then gulped at its size. At least 9 inches, it was by far the largest she'd ever seen. She wrapped her hand as far around it as she could; not even three quarters. Looking up at the older man's eyes as they bore into hers, Olivia began to gently stroke the massive cock in her hand.

"Fuck... You're so big Mr. Hoyt. Biggest I've ever seen," Olivia praised.

"Taste it," David said in a soft, but authoritative tone.

Olivia, tongue out, brought her head towards the married cock she held. She moved her head passed it and started at the base. Gently bringing her tongue to the bottom of the tool, then sliding it slowly up towards the tip, wrapping her lips around its head, then using her tongue to circle it, stroking the whole time. Her bright blue eyes never leaving David's, Olivia began to slowly bob her head down the enormous cock, that already filled her young mouth.

Tilting his head back briefly, David breathed out, "Oh fuck," before bringing his eyes back down to the teenage girl who had his cock in her mouth. "You like that, don't you Olivia? You little slut. You love sucking that big cock you've been teasing all day."

Olivia, bringing her head back to take a breath, teased back, "Yes, Mr. Hoyt. You taste so fucking good. You like having your little teenage neighbor suck your massive married cock?" then brought her lips back to bob back and forth again.

"Fuck that's so good, baby. God damn it. Olivia that's so fucking good. Just like that, you perfect little slut," David moaned out. He gathered a handful of Olivia's messy blond hair in one hand and used it to gently push his rock-hard prick further in, towards the back of the teenage girl's throat.

Olivia's eyes started to water, but she fought against the urge to pull away, allowing David to push deeper and deeper, until he started to hit the back of her throat. Olivia gagged, and pushed off for a second, then purposefully came back to take him into her mouth again, repeating the process over and over. Finally, after a few minutes, she becomes accustomed to the size and was able to take it more fluidly. It didn't take long for David's cock to start twitching in her mouth. Olivia got ready for what she knew was about to happen, but instead, she felt David yank her hair back off his cock. With a huge breathe in; he stayed calm while holding himself back from cumming.

After he'd regained control, David looked back down at the girl on her knees in front of him. "Stand up," he instructed. Smiling up at the muscular older man, Olivia pushed to her feet. David pulled her close, seemingly to kiss her, then roughly turned her around and pushed her over, so that her chest was pressing into the bed but she-ass was still pushed out towards him. After raising his right hand, David brought it down sharply onto the teenage girl's right ass cheek, drawing a surprised cry from Olivia.

"You like that, don't you, my little slut?" David growled out, bringing his cock close to Olivia's pussy, and running it up and down her slit. "You know you shouldn't be here. Now you're going to pay for it," giving her another sharp slap on the same cheek.

After a short recovery, Olivia smiled again, and said, "Yes Mr. Hoyt. I know I deserve it." This only bought another rough hand against her ass. Olivia cried out again and bit her lower lip in pleasure. She could feel her ass burning. "More Mr. Hoyt. Please... Punish your spoiled little whore."

"Good girl," David groaned out, bringing a gently hand down to massage Olivia's punished skin. Still rubbing the head of his cock against the young girl's soaking pussy "Guide me into you, Olivia," David said in a voice that refused to be questioned.

"Yes, Daddy," Olivia moaned out, preparing herself, and reaching under her to grip the older man's pulsing cock. She positioned it gently and started to push herself back against it, letting out a long moan as the head began to fill her. "Oh god, that's so good, Mr. Hoyt."

David took Olivia by the hips and started to push himself further in, closing his eyes and exhaling with pleasure. "Fuck, you're so tight, baby," he groaned out, pulling back. Agonizingly slowly, David pushed his cock in and out of the young girl, going an inch further each time, and drawing whines of pleasure from Olivia, until she buried her head in the mattress to stifle her cries.

David's pace started to pick up, his grip on Olivia's hips tightening, pulling her back against him more and more forcefully with every thrust. Olivia's whines grew into wails of absolute ecstasy as the married man behind her, drove himself into her tight young slit.

"Oh, fuck yes! Harder, Daddy! Use your little girl! Fuck that's so good, Mr. Hoyt! Fucking take your little slut!" Olivia encouraged, begging the older man for more.

David, hotter than his wife had ever gotten him, sped up his pace, driving his cock in and out of the high school girl he'd ached after for years, pushing with enough force to start moving the bed off its frame. When Olivia, crying out every time David's groin slapped against her ass, tried to bury her head back in the mattress, the man using her like a fuck doll, grabbed a handful of her golden hair and yanked her head back.

"I want to hear your moans, Olivia," David said, maintaining his pace and force, and drawing loud cries from the teenage girl on the end of his cock.

Growing tired, David's tempo started to slow, and his breathing picked up. He pulled back and, panting, said, "Get on your back, baby."

Olivia, desperate to make her married neighbor happy, crawled over to the pillows at the head of the mattress and, laid on her back, knees bent, and legs apart. David moved quickly on all fours, over to her, and repositioned himself at his stunning teenage neighbors opening. He leaned down towards her, one hand next to her head, and the other gripping the top of the headboard, and after a second of taking in Olivia's piercing blue eyes, David pressed his lips lustily against the young girls beneath him. After a few seconds, David began to push the head of his cock back inside his Olivia's wet pussy. She gasped, breaking the kiss, and then let out a low moan, her arms wrapped around David's body pulling him into her. David started to pick up his pace again, with long, smooth strokes, spurred on by Olivia's desperate squeals of absolute euphoria.

"Daddy, I'm gonna cum again! Cum with me, Daddy!" Olivia wrapped one arm around the back of David's neck, pulling his head down so Olivia could force his eyes to hers. "I want you to cum inside me. Please, fill me up Daddy. Fill up your little slut!"

David's breath became ragged and his strokes came with more and more force. Staring into Olivia's deep blue eyes, and with ecstasy that only years of torment can build, David moaned out, "I'm gonna fucking cum, baby! Fuck yes! Oh, Christ, you're so incredible! I'm gonna fucking cum inside you! Oh, fuck Olivia! Yes!"

With twin, continuous, howls of pleasure and satisfaction, David began to fill Olivia's teenage pussy with his seed, just as an orgasm had started to shake her body. David collapsed face down on top of her, his cock still inside of Olivia, both of them smiling, and panting to catch their breath.

After pushing himself off of her, David lay on his side next to Olivia, running a loving hand down her slim, toned body, and said softly, "I can't believe that just happened... Fuck Olivia, you're incredible... I can't believe... That was amazing."

Olivia gave a short giggle and said back, "You have no idea how long I've wanted that. It was better than I'd ever imagined," giving David a short kiss. Olivia lay there looking at David's weathered, and rugged face, running her small, soft hands over his chest and toned midriff, and then whispered, "I should go..."

After a pause, David whispered back, "I know...""I want to see you again. You know you still haven't danced for me," his teasing smile getting Olivia to blush and look down.

Olivia gave another giggle, "Next time then... I promise. I'm right next door if you need me." She gave her married neighbor another kiss, this one slightly longer, then she stood up and started putting her clothes back on. "I better get out of here quick," Olivia laughed. "Could be awkward running into Alexa on the way out."

David stared at the teenager he'd just had, as she got dressed. When Olivia was ready, he put on a robe and walked with her downstairs, getting her shoes for her from the hallway that she'd so expertly teased him in. Kissing her goodnight, he closed the door behind her, already wondering when he'd be alone with her again, praying it was soon.

Olivia rushed away from the house, terrified that a neighbor might see her leave. When she felt far enough away, she slowed down and started walking back to her car. She hoped that her parents would be asleep by now. She didn't want to see anyone else for the rest of the night.

Olivia had been eighteen all day, but now, she finally felt like an adult. There was a tiny twinge of guilt in her stomach when she thought about her friend Dana, David's wife Alexa, and her own boyfriend Matt, but more than anything Olivia was proud of herself. The way David had looked at her after, was something she'd never forget, and something she hoped to have a lot more of over the next few months before she'd have to leave for school.

Olivia made it to her car and drove home. Walking in the door, she saw that all the lights were off. She made her way upstairs, stripped off her clothes, and put on her soft pajamas. Olivia crashed onto her bed. Before long, sore and exhausted, she started to drift off. Before she finally gave in to her fatigue, Olivia's last thought was about how nice it would be to have Mr. Hoyt, muscular chest bare, lying next to her. There was no doubt in the eighteen-year old's mind, someday she'd make that happen. She couldn't wait.

116

# MY BEST FRIEND KAYLA'S BROTHER

My best friend Kayla's brother, Ben, has always had a crush. He is a young father, at thirty-six. When he was eighteen, he had Kayla's mom pregnant, so the fact that he's so young also means he's a little better than the rest of the kids. For years, I needed him, but it wasn't like I was over-running with chances to do something about that. All this improved during the winter break, to my great delight.

I have been going to college and staying with Kayla since September. At the University that we go here in Pennsylvania, we share a dorm room. When the winter break comes, which necessitates us to abandon our dorm, I decided that instead of moving to the part of the country where my mother and stepfather had moved to this time, I would just go home with Kayla and enjoy a week with her and her father. Once Kayla was five, Kayla's mom left so it was just her and her brother. Ben is a great parent who lets Kayla live her own life, but she is still motivated to be healthy. The fact that you can do anything to him is one of those things that made me fond of him.. Kayla and I are nearer than close, and since we were around fifteen anyway, I have pretty much lived in their place, and bringing me in the house is never a big deal.

We returned home for break the first night, Ben allowed us to have some friends around to hang out space in the basement to target pool. We are only eighteen, so procuring many bottles of wine wasn't a problem. We'd just enjoyed a couple of pool games before almost all wanted to go home. Some of the people there had been driving home from college that day for a couple of hours on the road so everyone was fairly bushed. Kayla's boyfriend Steve was the only one who remained.

We three went up to Kayla's room to chill and watch television. We shut off the lights, flipped on the TV and got comfortable. We crawled into her room, and I was at home on "my" bunk. It wasn't even midnight yet, but the alcohol had left me kind of lethargic, and I think they thought I was unconscious when I stopped speaking. It took just barely a few minutes before the sounds of them kissing filled the whole air. I can't lie, it's been a couple of weeks since I had sex last, and the noises that they made turned me on. I nearly moaned out loud myself when I heard Kayla asking Steve to kiss her cunt. I knew I needed to get out, or I risked letting them know how I was turning on. Fortunately, my bed was near the door, so I got up quietly and left. Looking back as I closed the door, I can see Steve directly between the legs of Kayla.  My eyes were going up to her face and I saw her smiling at me. I made a gesture of "I'm going downstairs" and she nodded.  I heard her give a deep moan just as the door closed shut. Looks like I got out just in time!

I started making my way back down to the basement. I thought I'd turn on the television and go to the sofa to sleep. When I got to the top of the stairs in the cellar, I knew the TV was already on. I figured Ben was already down there and my stomach flickered with little butterflies at the idea of spending a couple of minutes with him. I had a small, pink nightgown, and I asked if he needed it. I noticed the rhythmic thumping sound of quickened breathing as I came to the last few steps, along with the sound of Kayla's bed screeching on the floor above us. Imagine my surprise when I got out of the stairwell and saw Ben's hand jerking slowly up and down his dick!

I shrank a little further and sunk and I sat down in the darkness of the steps. Ben's cock was all I had expected, and much more. Around half-light, it looked so beautiful. His jeans were unbuttoned to allow his cock to hang freely, but he was still dressed in full. He was so goddamn hot, tossing his head to the back as he stroked his thick shaft. I heard Kayla scream again from above and remembered that the heating vent from the basement leads straight into her bed, which implied that we might hear all that was happening in her room.  When Kayla moaned or the bed squeaking picked up, I couldn't help but notice that the pace with which Ben worked at his cock did likewise.

Watching him move up and down his cock made me so horny, I could feel my slippers flooding with my cum. I couldn't turn away and while he rubbed himself I had to touch myself. I maneuvered a little to get my slippers off and put them on the stairs behind me. I watched as he continued stroking his hard dick up and down and I slipped my hand down to my clit. I was quite drenched, as soaked as I ever recalled being. I moved my completely soaking pussy with two thumbs, showing the sensation of moist hotness, giving my pussy some strong thrusts of my fingertips. I was so hot that I could feel my cunt while fingering myself.

I was very hot and horny, but I knew it was not the way I wanted to cum. Not tonight. It took me about a split second to make the decision which changed everything. I picked up my dress above my shoulders, brushed my fingertips through my hair, and walked into the basement nude.

Ben was still focused on his dick and I could see a shade of sweat on his forehead. He did not see me coming toward him with his eyes shut and his head tossed back. He didn't even know that I was there until I appeared before him. I leaned forward and snapped my hair in his embrace, and his eyes flew open. He wheezed for a second, who seemed to be ready to finally say something when I placed my fingertips in his mouth and said, "shhh." I could just see the moment when he turned away from my face and saw that I was stark naked. His heart sank and his cock had given a small little pre-cum when I gazed. I gave him a smile as I sank to my knees and said, "Is this for me?" As I bent forward, he let out a surprised groan and I began to lick his cock's tip.

I licked the whole of the shaft, including all over the head, pleased at being able to finally touch Ben the way I had always desired. There wasn't one inch of his gorgeous cock I hadn't licked before finally taking it into my mouth.

I looked up at him when I slipped my mouth over the ear and winked. Obviously, that was all the motivation he wanted. He put his hands in on either side of my neck, pulling it back so he could watch him show me the eye. I wasn't wasting time getting down to some rough biting, driving him down my throat so far as I can take him, dragging him back from time to time to spit on the clogged purple head before swallowing his thick shaft again. I was gathering speed and I could feel him breathing. I slid down my fingertips to my wet snatch and fingered myself for a second before bringing my hand to his lips. As I did so, he felt like he might burst. Having him lick my juices off his fingertips as I sucked his dick was one of the hottest and the best things that ever happened to me, the two of us maintaining eye contact as we did. The sound of Kayla and Steve above us, both moaning earnestly now as they pounded got me more than ready to get fucked.

He told me to get up and straddle his neck. Crouching on top of him, I bent forward and said, "Ben put that cock in me.

He wasted no time doing just that, taking my thigh with one hand and pushing his dick in with the other into my moist cunt. He was inside me, in one quick thrust, almost the whole way. I continued bobbing up and down, still crying. This position helped him to touch me at All right place and I could feel my pussy flowing to him juice. It took one or two minutes, but I was able to get all his cock into me early. Now I could feel the tip of his cock touching my cervix, so fucking good!

I started to raise myself as far as I could before repeatedly impaling myself on his shaft. He grabbed my face and pulled me forward for a hug, and we both began to make out. There was no passionate touch here. This was two men banging each other out of the hell too heavy to do it any other way. His hips were rammed up with each dorsal thrust I made, and I would moan deeper into his mouth every time that happened. I wasn't concerned that Kayla would hear us because the goddamn noise symphony that went on above meant that nobody was attentive to what we were doing.

I felt like I was about to get cum, so I pulled my lips away from him, sucking for air. "Fuck me, Ben, I'll cum," I muttered. He grinned at me as he put his fingers down to my pussy and started fingering my clit as I rode hard on him.

I could feel Kayla leaning over us, urging Steve to fuck her harder, the bed banging louder and louder against the wall. Each time she asked to be better fucked, Ben would drive in on me harder. I threw my head back and shrieked as I came, with one more fast thrust and his fingertips continuing to penetrate my clit. I came and fell and he never started fingering my cunt or sucking my clit. I was riding him still with enjoyment half out of my head. Suddenly, Ben caught my head and said, "I'm going to cum Tiffany! Where do you want it?" I knew exactly where I wanted it, and I wasn't wasting any time saying, "Cum in my pussy Ben! I want you to cover me with your fuckin' cum!" That seemed to drive him on even more, and I stared in shock as he kept pushing in on my cunt,  his face completely covered by sweat. The feeling that I had when his cum began showering my pussy inside was like nothing I've ever imagined. I could feel it entering my vagina, and I was sent off to another climax just realizing it was Ben filling me in with spunk.

Ben grabbed my face in his hands and put me in his mouth, slamming me in as we were both close to cumming with me hanging on his neck as if my life depends on it. My own cum dripped rapidly and violently out of me, and the sensations persisted and continued. I heard Kayla crying upstairs, "I'm cumming!" and I was pleased with the sound cover that she provided as our bodies smashed and Ben moaned to my mouth loudly.

I was a bunch of frail bones when we were finished. Completely exhausted, I still lie in me with him, bending forward and positioning my head on his shoulder. His palms were running up and down my back when I felt him laugh. "We will do THAT again SO!"

# WHILE THEY WERE SLEEPING

Katie glanced at Dr. Anderson as he rubbed his spouse's back. He winked at her as he moved her hair off the shoulder, tracing the slope of her neck along with his thumb. He had unbuttoned his shirt sooner or later and she or he was having a difficult time looking away. He has become well built, long hands and lean body, the small amount of his chest she ought to see turned into the described and smooth.

Mrs. Anderson sat on the ground along with her returned toward his knees, face slack and eyes at the TV. The smooth blue mild of the display flickered across her face as her eyes fluttered lazily. Her head rolled softly to the facet and Dr. Anderson leaned ahead and began to kiss the curve of her neck, shifting his hand down her chest and caressing her breasts.

Katie shifted barely and took in a deep breath. Her stomach clenched and her nipples tightened at the sight of him caressing his wife. Pulling a blanket over her chest, she wanted, she had now not shed her bra earlier than settling down for the movie.

Looking around the room, she noticed the alternative ladies were asleep. Melissa, Dr. Anderson's daughter, and Courtney, his niece, have been both loud night's breathing softly on the sofa beside her, their heads lower back, mouths open, legs tangled on the ottoman in the front of the sofa. Their sleepover appeared to be a bust.

Mrs. Anderson's head fell back on her shoulders and she or he began to snore softly. Dr. Anderson stood, picked his spouse up and gently placed her on the end of the section wherein he had sat. After she tucked her fist below her chin and pulled her toes collectively comfortably, he turned around and stretched.

Katie observed his erection jutting out below his gray paintings slacks, his white button-down falling open exposing his company flat stomach. He had seen her note him and he or she glanced shyly away.

"It seems we're the most effective ones awake." A playful grin cracked his generally stern face and he walked over to her. Katie attempted to sink further into the bend of the couch, pretending to watch the television. He knelt at the ground in the front of her and started to tug the blanket from her legs.

"You just had your 18th birthday. How do you feel at 18? An adult now ..." He slid his palms over her knees, digging his thumbs into his tender flesh of her internal thighs.

"What?" Katie gasped and pulled her legs up to her chest. "What are you doing?"

"You've been looking at me ... I've been looking at you." He wrapped two sturdy arms around each ankle and started to tug her legs in the direction of him.

"Right?" A half-smile cracked his face as he watched her, enjoying her trepidation, her legs resisting.

" No ... don't! She whispered quickly and tried to pull her feet back, but he grabbed it easily.

"If you like ... they may not wake up." He jerked her toward him and she or he slid forward, her hips preventing on his naked stomach. A sensation rushed via her and he or she felt her pussy moisten. Quickly, he wrapped his arms around her waist and began to kiss her aggressively, one hand sliding to the back of her head even as the alternative slide down her again and held her tightly to him.

She struggled for a moment, however, she soon felt her body soften. He became so tough in opposition to her, his arms so strong and fierce in her hair. His tongue licked hungrily in her mouth, and a strangled moan escaped her throat. She surrendered for a while, allowing her waist to sway on his stomach, and her thighs loved his side for care. He broke the kiss and smiled at her.

"That's right ..." He purred. He accumulated a fist complete of her hair and pulled her head lower back to have a look at him. "You've been looking at me for a while, haven't you? Tell the truth."

"Yes." She whispered. A hand slid around her stomach, lifting her skinny T-shirt. He ran his thumb lightly over her nipples and smiled, feeling stiff with his touch.

"Do you like me?" He grabbed her little breast and massaged roughly. She rolled her hips toward him, biting her backside lip and moaned "mmm hmm."

"Take your blouse off." He breathed. When she did not move, his eyes became stern and he growled "Now."

Katie obeyed and pulled off her blouse nervously, exposing her small white breasts to him. Unbuttoning his cuffs, he watched her and set free a hungry breath "You're so fucking sexy."

After pulling his personal blouse away, he bent to consume her, taking each breast in his mouth in turn, pulling her nipples with his teeth. She felt a wetness hose down her panties. Goosebumps protected her pores and skin as his tongue flicked tenderly over her nipples.

"Have you notion of me while you contact yourself?" He requested, straightening up and pulling her head to the side, smiling at how easy it was to handle her.

"How did you know?" Her voice was hoarse; breathless and scared. He dropped his hand to slip lightly alongside her inner thigh, his hands, locating her panties and smoothly slipping below the fabric.

"You look away when I have a look at you. You leave the room quickly after I come in. A rambunctious energetic girl will become shy and silent after I am around." He continued to kiss her neck as he spoke, his hands gambling along her sex, spreading her lips, feeling her wetness. "Ah, see ... You do want me, don't you? You have been looking at me tonight, secretly wanting me, haven't you?"

She smiled shyly and bit her bottom lip. He gave a low growl as he let to of her head, pressed her into the bend of the sofa and speedily pulled her shorts and panties from her legs, casting them to the floor.

"We can't ..." Katie tried to sit up, however, he positioned a big hand on her chest. "They'll wake up." She looked over at her friends; his daughter, his niece. They lay only some feet away, dozing deeply.

"They might not wake up." He murmured as he moved decrease, his eyes fixed on her uncovered wet pussy. "Be as loud as you need."

"No!" Katie said firmly, sitting up speedily before he could forestall her. "They are right there ... "

"Don't worry ... I gave them something to sleep." His darkish eyes glittered as he smiled up at her. "Now relax. Sit back. I may not let you know again."

Katie seemed over the room at his snoozing circle of relatives. She had an idea of him serving ice cream earlier, bringing each of them a bowl. "You drugged us?" She whispered.

"Them. Just something to sleep." He gently pushed her to go into reverse and started out to pry her knees apart, his voice developing stern. "As I said, I'm now not going to tell you again."

He diminished his head and positioned his mouth on her pussy, his tongue rolling over her clit and diving among her lips. A moan forced itself from her mouth as her back arched in satisfaction. He raised his eyes to observe her stomach and breasts rising with each motion of his tongue, her head rolling to the aspect with little moans. He inserted an extended finger and watched her mouth open wide, her forehead crinkling in tension, her knees drawing up round his ears.

"It's too much," she panted. His tongue rolling through her was more than she had ever felt, and she or he gasped on the pleasure spreading via her belly. "Stop, forestall."

He lifted his head and grinned, pulling her upright to him, kissing her forcefully.

Tasting herself on his lips gave her a brand new surge of satisfaction and she or he rolled her hips on to his finger and then dipped his finger inside her. He pressed some other long finger in and he or she whimpered softly. He made his head return fast.

"Are you a virgin?" He purred, a sluggish gleeful smile sliding throughout his face.

She nodded slightly, peering up at him apprehensively. He bent and kissed her extra lightly now, his palms sliding inside and out of her slowly, his thumb circling her clit. He strengthened his grip on the return of her neck, his thumb pressing behind her ear, rubbing the muscular tissues slowly. Her soft whimpers died and she or he started rolling her hips, her slim passage loosening round his fingers as a swell of delight grew. She began breathing heavily at a few meters away from his mouth while the moaning was on the higher frequency.

He broke the kiss lengthy sufficient to whisper "I'm going to fuck you tonight, child girl" as he quickens his pace, circling her clit together with his thumb and urgent his hands deep inside her. "Do you need to experience me inside you?"

"Yes," she breathed between groans, her head, pushing in opposition to his grip, hips shaking.

"Does this feel good, toddler girl?" His voice turned into gentle but stern, she heard a growl under each breath, and she unfolded wider for him. He quickly hand fucked her using his fingers, quickly flipped her clitoris with his thumb and choked.

"Oh yes, oh God yes" she whimpered, her legs shaking as a hurry of pleasure over got her and he or she cried out, orgasming on his fingers in quick quaking jolts.

"Oh fuck yes" he breathed as he felt her body convulse among his palms, her tight pussy spasming around his arms, her returned arching and her head falling limply lower back over her shoulders. "Cum, infant girl, cum for me" he growled, his cock throbbing in need for her tight virgin cunt.

He heard his spouse sigh softly in her sleep, transferring her legs in restlessly. Quickly and without expecting her small body to relax, he flipped her over, her belly toward the edge of the couch, her head buried in her arms, again and ass. Nevertheless, she is trembling with orgasm tremors. Releasing the cock from his pants, he spread her legs and pushed his penis head into her wet opening. A low soft moan got here from her and she pressed her hips lower back in the direction of him, lifting her ass encouragingly.

He started to fill her along with his long, tough cock, inch via inch, driving deeper into her virgin cunt, stretching it while he circled his hips. He grunted and groaned with the effort, digging his hands deep into the flesh of her thighs as her tight muscle mass squeezed his shaft. He growled and threw his head back, slowly pulling himself out and driving in again. Small whimpers and moans fluttered from beneath her hair, her ass rising and falling with every stroke.

"You ok, baby girl?" He whispered breathlessly, sliding a hand up her again and rubbing the back of her neck, tracing the slope of her shoulder.

"Mmmm hmmm" she moaned, her fists clutching the sofa as he drove into her with extra force. She set free a small cry, followed by a gentle moan. He paused, slipped on her back and wanted to open her as much as he did. He held her waist firmly as he glided returned in, spreading her legs wider as he did so. She shuddered slightly, her breath catching in her throat.

"Do you like that?" He requested to know, lifting her hips to take him easier. When she nodded, he started a consistent rhythm, driving his cock deeper. Her short and whimpered breaths soon became low candy moans of delight. With every deep thrust, he squeezed her hips, pulling her returned onto his cock.

He felt his orgasm begin to rise, the tightness of her virgin cunt, bringing him speedily to the threshold. When she reached back to maintain his forearms with two smooth palms, he lost manipulate and exploded deep inside her, coating her clean cunt with hot ropes of cum.

"Oh fuck yes," he grunted as he wrapped long arms around her shoulders, driving his cock as deep into her tight cunt as he in all likelihood could. He growled loudly, bucking into her ass with every flood of seed.

She let out a pointy cry as his cock impaled her, pushing against the touchy barrier within. The thickness of his cock, the constant pressure to her cervix, and the sharp ache of her walls being stretched mingled to push a new wave of ecstasy via her belly. Gripping the sofa in her fists, she wailed in delight and ache as an orgasm wracked her body.

Dr. Anderson leaned returned and groaned loudly, pulling Katie's hips lower back as he enjoyed the sensation of her quivering thighs, her cries muffled through the sofa, her cunt pulsing around his cock. Sliding his hands over her back and hips, he breathed softly "Good girl". She launched the tension in her again and melted into the sofa.

He massaged her lower back and shoulders, breathing deeply and playing the soft feel of her skin. Slowly he vacated her and bent to kiss her, chuckling at the little shivers his lips produced.

"What caused that?" She asked as she rose to her elbows.

"That, sweet girl," he massaged her hips, pressing inward and squeezing the gentle flesh of her inner thighs "become your first orgasm."

He became his head as Mrs. Anderson groaned in her sleep. However, the two girls still lay motionless at the sofa beside them. He smiled devilishly as he pulled Katie up from her reverie, cupping her small breasts as he whispered into her ear "Would you want a bath, infant girl?"

She smiled dreamily for a moment earlier than murmuring "Mmmm, yes."

Katie lay in a heat bath, her knees above the layer of bubbles and listened as Dr. Anderson carried his slumbering circle of relatives to their beds. Her pussy ached and the cleaning soap stung slightly, however, the warm temperature become soothing. She remembered his mouth to the clitoris and smiled, laughing with her arms running along her stomach.

When she stood up, he was watching her from the doorway, wearing most effective his boxers and smiling mischievously at her.

"Your appearance is so delicious," he purred and crossed the large master toilet to her, sliding his boxers down as he did. Katie smiled at him and dipped in warm water. "Let's make a room," he ordered, slipped behind her and calmed her between her legs. Immediately, his arms caressed her body, tracing her curves

"How do you feel?" He requested, sliding a gentle hand between her legs and caressing her mound with tender arms.

She gave a small shrug "It hurts a touch."

"Mmmm, I took you more difficult than I ought to have." He started to kiss her neck, his arms moving over her stomach and breasts. "You'll be sore for some days ... however, then, I'll have you ever again ... And again ... And again." With each kiss, he bit her neck, dragging his enamel softly over her pores and skin. She gasped a bit and squirmed underneath his fingers.

"I don't know," she muttered, thinking of her friend sleeping in the next room, and his wife was just outside the door.

His hands rose her throat and turned her face toward him. The other hand reached out between her legs and pressed her clitoris firmly, twisting her. "Don't make a mistake, baby girl ... you're mine now." He kissed her hard, gently pinched her clitoris, tense her thighs and kinked herself. She groaned in his mouth. He smiled and whispered, "This is just the beginning."

# MY BEST FRIEND'S FATHER

It became overdue. I didn't need to visit Jonsey's. However, I had no choice. I could not cross domestic after that. I could neither face my mom nor my dad. The argument was too much. There'd be no way I'd pass, crawling back after promising them that I would not want them. They stated I wouldn't last a week. I doubted I'd even remain a day....

I knocked on Jonsey's door lightly, understanding that he'd be wide awake. Jonsey would be up at this time, working on his drawings. He became a hentai obsessive and was quite appropriate at it too. What amazed me was that his bedroom light wasn't on. Usually, his mother and father would be downstairs, so he would stay upstairs and draw, but I figured they must have gone to bed. I was so nervous. What might I tell James and Sonya if they requested to know what I was doing here?

The door opened, eventually, and I became prepared to hug Jonsey and beg him to let me live for multiple days till my dad and mom stopped being dicks, however, rather than my brief, plump friend, I was greeted by the tall and muscular built of his dad.

"Gabrielle?" He requested, a bit confused. I forced a grin as he stood to put on the porch light.

"Yeah, sorry to trouble you like this, Mr. Jones, however, I just want to see if Jone and Tom were in," my tone was shaking, I started trembling from the bloodless and nervous thinking about what James's reaction would be.

"No, sorry! In the long past, Tom lived with his grandmother along with his mom. She's now not properly taken care of, so Sonya's took him there." My heart sank. I thanked him and bade him goodbye, geared up to walk home defeated. Then his voice stopped me.

"Why did you need to look him, besides?" I came around, my hair damps from the earlier rain and my garments were sticking to me.

"I've had....an argument with my dad and mom and I turned into simply...wondering...whether I should stay with you," I smiled a bit and grew to become again spherical. "Never mind, I'll be high-quality."

I heard the door close, sighing disappointingly. I knew that James wouldn't let me stay without Jonsey there, however, I hoped. I started feeling sorry for myself again, on foot fast away, till I felt a hand on my shoulder. I jumped lower back, startled, to find myself searching into the face of my satisfactory friend's father.

"Stay if you need," James whispered, his words best clearing moments after.

"N..No, thank you, I don't want to impose." I found myself staring at Jonsey's father, wondering why he seemed so beautiful to me, and why exactly he did not mind me staying.

"Seriously, Gabrielle, live. I cannot pressure you back, I've been drinking. I don't need you going domestic now because it's too overdue and what will one, or a couple of nights be? Tom's room is loose. But we have a spear beside." He smiled at me, his smile candy and heat. I discovered myself agreeing, returning his smile nearly flirtatiously, although now not pretty sure why....

James let me into the house, leaving the door of the living room open for me, most effective to run in before me once he realized he'd left his video on. I smiled as I noticed the women who liked some large bodybuilders' balls. James checked me out again, blushing.

"Sorry," he muttered, embarrassed and jogging returned to me to take my coat.

"I'll get you a towel, to, erm, dry off," I found myself looking him disappear up the stairs clutching my coat. I stood in the doorway for a moment, frozen, pretty uncertain what was going on, until I heard James, commanding me to sit down and make myself feel at home.

I sat returned, nonetheless, a little dazzled as a result of what happened. And James... I smiled a touch, remembering how adorable he'd appeared when he blushed....

While awaiting James to return, I discovered myself looking at the family pics which I'd seen a thousand instances before. Several of Jonsey. The bare baby images which all of us dread. A couple of James, Sonya and Jonsey, even a few of me and Jonsey as kids, however none of James and Sonya collectively.

I shook away the thought, smiling at James as he got here down the steps, preserving a red cotton towel.

"Is this ok?" He asked, his voice breaking my concentration on the pictures.

"Eh, yeah, great. Thank you once more, Mr. Jones." He sat next to me on the sofa, passing me a towel and coyly lifting the remote manage to flick on a random song channel.

"Don't worry. I've regarded you for a while now, Gabrielle. If there are ever any problems, come here. I virtually don't mind." I stared at him for a moment, while patting my hair with the cotton. He put on a beautiful smile. His lips were complete and juicy. Now, I realized why Jonsey's lips were of the first-class quality, he inherited them from his father. I suddenly realized.

I realized that I had begun to fall for my first-class friend's father and I was desperate to have him.

I went back to patting my hair, realizing that I had started blushing now.

"Thanks, Mr. Jones. This means a lot."

"Call me James," he stated, growing and taking his wine glass. "You want a drink?" He stated, winking in the direction of the spirits cabinet. For a moment, I decided to tell him that I was underage, however, he knew. I smiled and nodded telling him I'd have something he had.

I lay the towel down and unzipped my boots, revealing my fishnet protected legs to my excellent friend's father. For a second, I tried to figure out whether or not James has been doing something earlier than I came. I puzzled whether he masturbated... Despite it being for a second handiest, I could not prevent deliberating how stunning he could have seemed... His hand tight around his erection, transferring up and down slowly, on his face a glance of natural ecstasy...

James's cough distracted me from my fantasy, my blush returning immediately.

"So, do you want to tell me what happened? I might be capable of help," I smiled for a second, mesmerized by way of his soft voice and piercing blue eyes. Nevertheless, I nodded and instructed James the entirety. I discovered myself telling my pleasant friend's dad matters that I would not even tell my high-quality friend, things so private and nearly disturbing which had made me cry myself to sleep on such a lot of occasions. And James understood it all. He even understood some of the things I did not.

I was determined, my eyes glued to his firm, spherical ass as he was given up and went into the kitchen to fetch any other bottle of wine. Damn, he was exceptional. Too pleasant.

"So have you obtained a boyfriend at the second?" He sat next to me and passed me the total glass, my palms going for walks over his as I took it off him. Jesus, this has to stop. I appeared away, however, only after taking a brief peek on the crotch of James's pants, both overjoyed and giddy by way of the mild bulge.

"Erm, no, now not at the moment," I observed that he grinned a touch as he added the glass to his lips.

"Tom, however, hasn't got a girlfriend, I'm guessing?" I laughed, thinking if he had meant to be so sarcastic.

"No, but I'm sure he is just saving himself for a special girl." He looked at me and shook his head, nevertheless, smiling.

"He desires you to be that woman. He thinks you are amazing. He always talks about you. Seriously! Is he in with a chance?" I lower back his gaze, our eyes locked for pretty a second earlier than my shaking voice broke the silence.

"We're too excellent friends, plus I've kinda been given my eye on someone else on this very second in time," I wondered if I hinted on who I have been virtually gazing at, and I questioned if James took the hint. He smiled and laughed a bit, whilst I, in the end, realized what he'd just stated.

"Are you serious? Tom desires us to date?" James laughed, shaking his head and his stray hair whipped his face lightly. I felt my body tingle as I watched his slightest movement. He appeared to have ignored my accidental hint, and in reality, answered my question.

"Would I deceive you? He's desired you when you consider that he is about 13. He's getting nowhere, is he?" I shook my head, drinking extra in amazement. I couldn't understand why.

"He still hasn't kissed a woman but? By the time I was his age, I had lost my virginity three times." I laughed, trying to prevent questioning bout James and myself...

"No, he hasn't," I whispered. His subsequent comment snapped me from my trance.

I felt James shift a touch next to me.

"Not had more good fortune than me then," he said, blushing a bit and smiling. I checked him out a bit confused, till my cheeks broke into a pink blush and I realized the thriller of my confusion.

"Oh, why, how long has it been?" It simply popped out. It was as if I became the spokesman to a friend, and any question was first-rate to ask.

"' About a year and a half, that's how long I found out she'd been with someone else." I gasped. James and Sonya were committed to having the right relationship. I continually envied Sonya, asking questions about how James became clearly lovely. "After that, I decided not to have anything doing with her again. We've been checking out the divorce papers for a while now." He paused, with his hands in his pockets.

"She took Tom to fulfill her new man," he pulled out a cigarette, followed by way of a lighter.

I sat speechless, best transferring to back far from the smoke.

"I have come to despise her. And she feels the same about me. She even hates the way I even have my hair now," he stated this laughing, causing my lips to twist into an innocent smile.

James really did not care anymore. There was no sadness, no regret in his voice, nor his eyes.

"Really? Well, it is stupid. You have beautiful hair." He laughed. But it was true, I had constantly loved James' hair. It was a dark brown color, nearly black. Usually, he'd brush the waves behind his ears and permit the rest of the gelled curls to bounce freely of his shoulders.

I discovered myself misplaced in my thoughts and moved in the direction of James, leaning over him and taking the cigarette from his hand.

"You should not smoke," I whispered, twirling my body around so I confronted him. He smiled at me, sliding down the couch so my head became brushing his chest as opposed to stomach. I felt my heartbeat begin to increase as I dropped the cigarette in the ashtray and certainly I felt my own hand flow up his chest, trembling. I sat on James now, one in all his arms around my waist and the opposite stroking my leg.

I could feel openings around my lips and my trembling hands desperately gripped his clothes. I sat there, nearly paralyzed as James's barely parted lips began to move closer and toward my own. My lips remained like that for a moment, my eyes staring into his until I observed myself giving into the outstanding temptation of my first-class friend's father. My lips parted a bit more, permitting his tongue to brush mine lightly and my eyes fell close. My shaking tongue began to respond, gliding over his masculine yet dreadfully soft one. He pulled me closer, causing my breasts to crush towards his chest. My own fingers began to discover his body after a couple of minutes of reassuring kisses.

I began to sense his maximum intimate part hardening, pushing hungrily against my top thigh as he cupped my breasts. Neither people had made an attempt to stop

this, in spite of both understanding that this was very wrong. For a moment, I started to marvel at what Jonsey could do if he knew that my legs were currently

being unfolded by his father's trembling palms. I pulled my mouth far away from James's, at the equal time wrapping my arms tightly around his neck, my breathing almost violently. I felt him pull his hand from underneath my skirt, after caressing my thighs teasingly. I felt his violent breaths on my neck, exciting me similarly, inflicting my complete body to tremble with anticipation. I had all started to get terribly moist. The silkiness in my pussy rubbed off on my pants.

"James," I whispered, jogging my tongue down his cheek, shivering slightly at the feel of his stubble against my tongue.

"Mmm?" I felt my hand slide into his blouse, hoping this will deliver him a slight hint that I wanted him greater than some things right now. I felt his breath on my neck as he laughed. I knew James hadn't done anything sexual for a while, nearly years, he'd said.

But as James took my hand and led me up the steps, kissing me each time his foot landed on a brand new step, it all regarded too right. We stumbled into the darkness of his bedroom, immediately falling onto the mattress, immediately tangling our bodies together.

He caressed my face as he laid me down, placing innocent kisses on my nose and lips as his palms slipped into my blouse, sliding his hand into my bra to caress my breasts slowly. He pinched my difficult nipples gently, at the same time as licking my neck and shoulders. My fingers slipped into his shirt, sliding down his smooth, nearly hairless chest. Our kisses became nearly violet now, a consistent tangling of our eager tongues. James's velvet tongue slid over mine, nipping it lightly on occasion as he positioned himself on the pinnacle of me, spreading my arms with the aid of my facets in a crucified position as he lifted my blouse a bit beyond my breasts and placed tiny kisses from my belly to my covered breasts. I may want to experience his erection pushing hungrily against

my legs, begging to be released. He pulled me up, his different hand pulling the shirt over my head. He dropped it beside me on the bed whilst his lips danced over my chest and the uncovered regions of my breasts.

I released mild moans, almost feeling vulnerable and completely at this beautiful guy's command. His stubble tickled my stomach, inflicting me to giggle barely as his hands glided up my thighs and under my skirt, removing my tights in an instant. He appreciated my legs proper as much as my thighs, preventing me to kiss my moist panties earlier than climbing back on the pinnacle of me. He ran his hands down my face, allowing his lips to caress every vicinity that his lips had just touched, causing my frame to dance in euphoric shivers. I felt myself wrapping my legs around his organization ass, my feet strolling down his slit joyfully. He applied weight to the arced arm while he was exploring the contents of my bra for disease with the trembling arm of the other hand. I felt his hot breath in opposition to my skin, my pussy trembling, as his arms pressed down on the tender silk of my breasts, traveling nervously to my nipple.

His eyes shut and he forced his lips upon mine, his index finger circling my tough nipple, forcing me to break out inside the diabolically impossible to resist shivers again. He started to take a seat up, pulling me up with him so our kiss would not be broken. He ran his tongue down my neck now, his palms sliding in the back of my lower back to take the barrier of my bra away, instantly freeing my breasts. He launched a pleasing groan, taking my breasts into his palms and massaging them slowly. He kissed each one, every nipple, then he drove me down once more. He eliminated my skirt in an instant, with no traces of hesitation. I discovered myself rolling onto him as he ran his thumbs around my nipples. I grinned at him, slipped his arm into his chest, then unbuttoned his shirt and slid it from his hand to show the beauty of bare breasts. I observed myself vulnerable to the temptation of contact, looking to feel that silky skin underneath my lips. I lowered my lips to his stomach, moving down softly as it tightened under my lips.

I heard him whisper something and circulate his hand into my hair as I began to lick up his chest, going for walks my enamel over his erect nipples lightly. I felt his different hand slide down mine again, pushing my nipples further into his belly.

I started out kissing his belly downwards, adoring the feel of his erection in opposition to my frame. My arms slipped into his jeans, playing with the button before ripping it off and unzipping the pants with my teeth. He chuckled softly at this, lifting his body at the same time as I pulled away from his pants. I climbed his frame, my nipples rubbing his thighs, his belly, his chest.....

I brushed my lips against his teasingly, only breaking into the entire kiss once he's pulled down my head and begun to kiss me passionately, nearly violently. His tongue slid over mine, examining, inflicting a whole and sensual tornado. I broke the kiss eventually, keen for greater air. As the candy nectar of the oxygen crammed my lungs, he flipped me onto my return, kissing my shoulders inside the progress. His arms cupped my breasts again as he began to slip down my frame, spreading my legs coyly.

I lay down now, my breaths nearly exhausted as his lips started to hint my neck and breasts, his hair tickling my chest and stomach as he slid himself down me, setting his lovely, muscular torso in-between my moist thighs.

His index finger traced my slit, the wetness lubricating it instantly. His warm breath on me induced me to shiver, building up my excitement earlier than ultimately giving into a noisy and lustful moan as his tongue slid around my clitoris, finding it instantly. He commenced circular movements, my frame tingling with pride as I wrapped my legs around his neck as he accelerated the pressure of his velvet tongue toward my clitoris, understanding this will deliver me to orgasm in seconds.

With every stroke of his tongue against my maximum delicate part, I moaned, groping the quilts violently, the quilts wherein he slept as soon as with his spouse. I felt my eyes fall shut in ecstasy, my hips rising and muscular tissues tightening, the room revolving around me, my thoughts nonexistent..... He leaked away my cum, comforting my aching clitoris together with his tongue again, before kissing each, he considered one of my legs and crawl up to me, leaving a wet trail of his saliva and my cum on my belly and breasts.

Our tongues danced once more, lightly, my palms scratching down his again to grab his tight ass as he slid in between my legs.

I gasped, feeling the tip of his lubricated, precum protected cock stroking my entrance, understanding his depraved intentions. I pressed one hand to his chest, transferring his body as far away as feasible from allowing his semen to come close to my juices. I moved his hair at the back of his ears, kissing his neck and shoulders.

"I'm sorry, I can't," I whispered, blushing barely, no longer wanting to peer at his reaction. He nodded, smiling sympathetically and catching my lips along with his very own.

I twirled his frame around, forcing him beneath me, trying nothing.

However, he is inside of me right now, knowing it became impossible. I ran my surrender his moist tip, tingling at the sensation of its exhilaration

underneath my touch. We kissed once more, his tongue weak. I kissed his muscle tissues, shifting down his frame slowly and seductively, growing the depth of my kisses. I sooner or later reached his erectness, the precumed tip glistening beautifully, the shaft, long and invincible almost, the balls, tight and smooth. His fingers buried themselves in my hair, pushing my head

lightly forward, my pouting lips in a kiss on his head. He twitched

below the smooth contact of my tongue, encouraging me, in addition, to run my tongue down the lengthy, difficult shaft. I took the top into my mouth, circling it with the tip of my tongue as I took greater of him in, knowing there could be no way I may want to take his fullness into me. My index finger moved in-between his balls, feeling them tighten deliciously below my touch, at the same time as I ran my tongue over his lubricated shaft again, causing almost an uproar of pleasant moans. With my free hand, I took his shaft, shifting choreographed with my tongue and mouth, my palms nevertheless walking over his continuously tightening  balls.  His body tensed,  his short,  sharp breaths transformed into long moans,  and eventually,  with  a  groan, his heated semen   squirted    into    my    mouth, causing me    to swallow quickly because of the amount.

After a second of cleaning his head, feeling his frame loosen up in utter utopia, I felt his robust arms pull me up to his lips, my mouth on his again, sweet kisses. His hands slid down my palms, onto me again, guiding me lightly to a harmless position, making him in control now. The velvet of his tongue slid down my neck, analyzing my entire frame, the kisses irresistible, from my lips to my thighs. Both of our bodies rubbed collectively, moist with sweat from our exhilaration. My body echoed with tiredness, having skilled pleasures it had in no way earlier than visible, and I instructed him so, to which he merely smiled.

A glass of wine curled up in his fingers and running his shoulder-length curls over my palms. I was in utter disbelief as I drifted off right into sleep. An argument with my dad and mom and several hours later falling asleep, naked, in opposition to my great friend's father. I felt James's lips hint mine before I, in the end, gave in to the exhaustion. I awoke, frowning and squinting immediately, feeling the rays of the sun against my unopened eyes. Stretching slightly, I opened my eyes and shifted to my proper, almost not anticipating him to be there, nearly believing the entirety to be a dream. Still, I smiled instantly as my eyes opened to a great portrait of my pleasant friend's father, my lover, mendacity, angelically along with his head urging softly in opposition to mine. His breathing was slow, deep, and his entire complexion peaceful as he slept. I blushed, taking one final observe him before running into the bathroom and releasing my bladder.

Guessing that James would not think, I organized a bathtub, slipping into it, overwhelmed with the aid of its heat. It was kind to my body, soaking my muscle groups within the most intimate ways.

My nonviolent utopia became interrupted by way of a knock at the door, for a moment, a horrible and fearful moment, I believed it to be Sonya, James's spouse of 18 years. Still, my fear was laid to rest as I found James standing in the doorway. How attractive he appeared now, his full weight leaning on the door frame, wearing only jeans.

"I'm just going down to get a few meal supplies. I'm hoping you'll stay tonight?" I nodded, returning his smile.

"All proper. I'll get a few matters to us then." He walked towards me, walking his hand via my wet hair as he reached me, and kissed my lips briefly.

"You have clothes here. It's in the spare room. Don't worry, I've not let Tom masturbate over them." I laughed, watching him leave slyly earlier than sinking lower back into my bath of heaven.

I had washed and changed and even organized a touch breakfast for myself. By the second hour of James's disappearance, I had begun to worry. An automobile pulled up within the power, commotion, a woman's voice. Shit. It could not be. I walked to the door nervously, geared up to sprint out.....

"What's the matter?" James said, instantly losing his luggage and coming to me to embody me. I buried my head in his chest, feeling the comfort of his body in opposition to mine. He kissed my hair, his contact comforting.

"Sonya may not be again 'until tomorrow. That became my neighbor I turned into talking to. Darling," he whispered, lifting my chin so my eyes have been looking deeply into his.

"Trust me."

We kissed. A simple day of conversation and kissing, so harmless and almost toddler-like groping, never bringing each other to orgasm at some point in the direction of the day. A had never skilled this kind of pleasurable

day. Neither of us had regrets about the events of the previous night, which amazed me. Still, James regularly reassured me that he wanted what was going on now if he failed to, he would have instructed me immediately away. I immediately knew that I'd found something else in James, something aside from only a guy who could

deliver me to a fantastic orgasm with just the electricity of his tongue. I observed a lover, a friend, a real man. A guy who I wanted to be with.

The day passed by too quickly.

"I don't want this to end," I whispered to James, going for walks my tongue down his ear.

"Me neither," he whispered, turning his head slightly and kissing me, our lips united as one, and handiest one. I stood up, understanding that this would be our final night time collectively till Sonya moved out. James had informed me that he desired to look me, to be with me, however, it was impossible for now. Until she moved away, besides. Then, we would have the problem of Jonsey to discuss. He promised me, promised me in his world, that we might be together soon. He stated we'd make it work if I truly wanted to. How could I no longer? I turned into besotted with James.

We found ourselves locked in every other hand soon sufficient, the flesh of our top bodies bare and glistening in sweat and saliva from the messy yet awfully irresistible kisses. James kissed in-between my breasts his fingers circling my nipples. The fake laughs of the cleaning soap superstars at the television made me shiver.

James lifted me off the sofa, put me down lightly onto the ground as though I was the maximum delicate flower. His massive hands slid down my body, forcing me to arch my back. I felt his long arms hint the define of my pants, sliding down into them teasingly before ultimately unzipping them and pulling them off me, kissing my thighs and his hands dancing gently up my legs, stroking my moist panties in a sweet and sensitive manner earlier than climbing again up my frame and helping his weight on his elbows. His hair brushed my cheeks and neck as we kissed, as his tongue slid over mine and my palms roamed his returned, pushing his buttocks down and feeling his erect shaft brush teasingly toward my sex.

My body tingled, causing me to break out into a smile and slide my palms down his chest to the button of his jeans. I felt his breaths growing in opposition to my skin, fast and arousing, as his lips came closer and closer to my neck. I pulled down the zip of his pants, bringing to life his rigid erection. He stood and slipped from his pants immediately, allowing me to move slowly to him and run my quit his boxer shorts, adoring the wet patches of the pre-cum. I cupped his balls, massaging them tenderly as his palms danced through my hair. I removed his boxers soon sufficient, instantly greeted by means of his glistening manhood. I took the top in my mouth, going for walks with my tongue over the small slit, taking in all of the pre-cum. My hand started to transport up and down his shaft, increasing the velocity as he multiplied his breaths. Then I subsidized away as I felt his frame, demanding up, equipped to release. Making certain I had kept off his arms, I stood up, kissing him before he could have the opportunity to protest.

"Did you purchase something?" I whispered to him, feeling his unsatisfied breaths on my neck. He looked up, his blue eyes looking over my frame, reassuringly.

"Yes, do you really want to?" I kissed him while sliding my palms down his again and lightly pushing his pelvis near my genitalia. "Yes."

"All proper," he whispered, kissing me and running his fingers over my body lightly. "Give me a minute." He bent down, finding his pants and searching through his pockets till his eyes met mine, satisfied, and keeping a tiny blue packet. He gently stroked my wet panties, resting his hand on my foot and resting his hand on his shoulder. "Put it on you," he whispered when he stood up. I took the small blue packet from him, ripping the edge eagerly and removing the round, lubricated condom. I stepped back a bit, making some area in-between me and James's erection, giving me sufficient area to slide it onto him with none frustration. I slipped it onto his shaft carefully, my frame tingling with exhilaration as he released a moderate groan. I took his hand in mine, leading him in the direction of the handiest wall now not adorned with cheesy flower paintings, spreading my body on it right away.

James started to kiss me, my neck, sliding his lips down my frame till his tongue reached my belly and his hands began to pull down my panties. I felt his finger trace my slit instantly, causing me to close my eyes and clutch his shoulder for the guide. He moved his face toward my aching intercourse, strolling his tongue down the slit, locating my clit instantly. He started to flick his tongue over its swollen body slightly, bringing me closer and in the direction of orgasm with every contact. Unfortunately, my heaven came quickly to life. He stood up again, wrapping one arm around my waist and the alternative on his shaft. I sensed his hand slipping through to support my bare ass. "Please wrap your feet," he whispered.

His other arm speedy lifted me, allowing me to do as he had ordered. I wrapped my hands around his neck for extra aid, trusting him absolutely with this new role to me. I threw my neck returned as he took his shaft, permitting the head to press in opposition to my clit earlier than ultimately thrusting deep inner of me. I moaned immediately, an aggregate of pride and pain.

He kissed my neck, adding extra centimeters to me. Two in, three out...

The moderate infection and pain immediately diminished and the simplest delight observed his thrusts. His pelvic bone rubbed towards my clitoris, increasing my possibilities of orgasmic pleasures. My lips parted in enjoyment, my breaths quickly growing and turning into moans as James's breath beat off my neck. I had never had such outstanding lovemaking. Never so gentle, so meaningful...

James lifted his face from my neck, bringing his lips to mine for a hungry kiss. I started to push him, in addition, into me, my frame begging to be released, my pussy aching in ecstasy. I felt my frame tightening eventually, all of my muscular tissues tensing, my breathing rapid and impatient....looking...

I screamed out his name, my frame immediately going limp in his palms. Every part of me from my feet to my fingers tingled in the most wonderful orgasm. It did not take James any longer to cum, his body tensing, his eyes closed in ardor before I felt him release, moaning in a most accomplished manner as we collapsed onto the ground.

I observed myself reluctant to having to permit the pass of James. Still, I knew too properly Sonya would be lower back early. And she did precisely that. I heard James arguing with her immediately, she was screaming at him for letting me live. Jonsey got here in the spare room, after telling his mother to shut up, and looked at me.

"They woke you up?" He asked, a dissatisfied look on his face. I smiled pulling the duvet over me, hoping that he hadn't seen me wearing one in all his father's shirts.

"No, I've been awake for a while." He rolled his eyes and came over, sitting at the bed.

"They will split up soon, you know. My mom's moving out in about 3 weeks," I did my best to hide my delight, not wanting to talk to Jonsey as I could not help but smile. I heard a slight knock on the door and James entered.

"Your mom's long past out Tom," he stated, his eyes locked with mine. I smiled at him, once more in amazement at how sexy he appeared in the most effective his black boxers. I remembered our night, and the way neither of us slept, how each time we went to bed one or the alternative could go again, breaking into uncontrollable passion immediately.

"Morning, Gabrielle. Sorry if I woke you," his smile remained, our eyes locked and I was hypnotized again by his voice.

James and I started a daring relationship, each time I stayed at Tom's (which I do plenty more now) I continually stayed within the spare room, and he paid quite a few visits to the toilet. He'd come spherical to mine, even for 15 minutes after school whenever my parents were at work. And we promised every difference

that this would be beyond a mere short term relationship, we both wanted

the actual thing. Sonya could pass out soon, after which I should have James all to myself...

# MY BEST FRIEND'S DAD

Being raised in a strict and religious home, I turned into pretty naive and harmless of intercourse, swearing, men, even alcohol - that was the case before I turned 19. We were imagining to go out for my 19th birthday, instead,

I was babysitting with my friend at her residence, looking after her younger

brothers and her parents had long gone out to have fun on the occasion of her Dad's (MrC) fiftieth birthday.

The family had had a massive marvel birthday the preceding weekend for him and all and sundry was satisfied at the occasion. They were good friends with my family. Anyway, we watched films practiced our dance habitual and talked till MrC and MrsC got here home.

When I went to the bathroom, I didn't know MrC was there, then I entered the bathroom and saw him rubbing his cock. I did not know what to say or do and I simply stared at it due to the fact I hadn't seen an actual one on a person before, then I quickly ran to the front room where my pal was and didn't say a word. I had by no means even seen my personal brother's or Dad's cock not to mention a cock on somebody else.

About five mins later, MrC got out and seemed surely irritated he told me to get my stuff collectively and he might drop me home. When we got to the corner just down the road, he told me I had become naughty and said that he noticed me looking at his cock and he asked if I appreciated it. I did not answer and just looked directly ahead, I was so surprised due to the fact that MrC is good friends with my Dad and I have regarded him for years like an Uncle. He asked me if I were with a person and I said no. I considered it as an abnormal question.

As he continued riding,  he was still talking about me gazing at his cock. Suddenly, he started touching me between my legs and sort of grabbed and squeezed at my crotch area. I moved as far as I could from him, right up toward the automobile door AND crossed legs firmly shut. He said that I have been staring at him for months and sporting small skirts deliberately, and he even said that I have been flashing my panties typically at him.

Flabbergasted at all of this, I denied it, I said all ladies wore small skirts and half tops;  it turned  into the fashion consisting  of his  daughter, my friend. He stated I  was a tease alright and he saved touching me in a bad place.  I said 'NO' sincerely loud, I  have  never  tried  this and I started  crying,  he stated that  I was up  for  it  and he said he should inform by  means  of the way I  dressed,  that  I  had teased him. I instructed him I didn't mean to but that made him angrier and  in  a split of  a  second, he  yanked  me near him on  the  front seat, pulled  up  my  skirt,  went straight internal my  panties  and turned into touching my pussy together with his finger.

I looked  at him  with  disbelief  and  hatred  and tried desperately to move away - we have  been going  too speedy for  me  to  jump out  of the car.  He  yelled  at  me  to  open  my  legs similarly aside for  him and said he was going  to  have some for  his  birthday.  I  refused  to open my legs and I did not circulate. He stated I turned into moist due to the  fact I desired him,  I told him  no!  No!  NO!, then  he  used his loose hand  to force my  legs apart and began jamming  his finger proper  inside  and  out  of  me, inside  and  outside, inside  and outside simply thrusting it in deep and I screamed at him to stop.

He told me I  was a fucking tease and he was going to teach me a lesson, I  yelled  "no"  and  said "stop, it  hurts, you  are hurting  me", but he went faster inside  and  out, in  and  out, in  and  out, inside  and outside, he said, "how  does  it sense to  fuck  an old man's  finger, you love it Rose you teasing whore". I  wasn't used to swearing and the words he was using, scared me. I tried to move his hand out of my panties.

150

However, he kept on moving into and out, in and out, in and out shoving it forcefully while I was trying to fight him off. I instructed him that I could tell Mrs. C. However, he laughed and said nobody would believe me and it WAS my fault for looking at him. He demanded to know what I turned into going to present him for his birthday and it needed to be special.

I attempted to crouch far away from him. However, he could not get his manic finger away from my vagina, in and out, "you love it, Rose, admit it, you wanna fuck, I'll show you how to fuck", in and out, inside and out. I begged him to stop, then he said he hadn't even commenced, and I got virtually scared, he said I had absolutely quality younger titties - I tried to fight him off, but in spite of his using one hand to drive and one hand in me he becomes too powerful to stop and it made him cross faster with his finger. He stated I was too young for him even though I had already clocked nineteen years.

However, he said he was going to teach me not to tease, I was happy I was too younger for him and desired him to stop.

I dug my fingernails into his penetrating hand which was pounding into my pussy and said 'you are hurting me badly I do not even use tampons, you finger hurts' then he slammed at the brakes he stated 'we will I'll hold that in thoughts

Rose, do not be scared' and earlier than I ought to assume he had absolutely moved me round at the seat on my return he forced my legs aside and put them either side of him. I couldn't move and I was terrified.

My leg was pressured within the air and against the roof, he smelt his finger then began poking me slowly inside and out, inside and out and his finger came out moist and he slid it around my pee-hole, and inserted his finger again inside me then back out and around my clit and in my vagina and backward and forward, again and again, and I quietened down and then he moved his head down near my pussy for a look, which I notion turned into bizarre.

But at that moment, for the first time, I felt something right, excellent his tongue was flickering all around my clit and among my lips, I became surprised. I appreciated this and it surely did feel excellent, I realized I made noise due to the fact he kept yelling at me 'you want it, don't you, you want it, you perving bitch' then his finger went in my pussy while he turned into licking my pussy, I almost died from pride, in and out actual and gradual and tongue going frantically round my clit, then he inserted his finger into my butt and I yelled in pain and pleasure as he licked tougher and faster and poked my different holes.

He kept yelling "you like it you little slut" and in the end, I moaned " yes MrC" then he sat up and I became so upset it had stopped due to the fact that I was throbbing from somewhere I had never been before - I desperately desired more. He called me a slut and a whore and told me to suck him off or he's going to tell my parents what I turned into. I had no concept that 'suck off' intended blowjob which I had heard of but by no means achieved, then he grabbed me so hard that my whole body was dealing with a different manner and I ought to feel my hair being pulled out of its roots.

I knew my face was in his crotch area. It made my pussy throb more, however, he stated I had to earn it and fuck him with my mouth. He manhandled his jeans fly with the problem and pulled his penis out of his pants and said 'deliver me a birthday present'. Right then it looked a way other than what I saw in the toilet and I seemed not to definitely understand what to do, he yelled at me to suck it now 'now Rose' and I'll take you home. Suck it all of the manners to your residence. So I just put the pinnacle element into my mouth and he started out up the car once more and started to drive, the guidance wheel dug into my head and all of the while he was yelling at me, he was impatient.

I wasn't doing it appropriately enough. However, I hadn't achieved it earlier than and I surely desired to delight him it supposed a lot to me, I tried very hard to suck his cock and then he grabbed my hair and pulled my head up and down truly hard onto his cock. I wasn't doing something he became just shifting my head up and down, up and down and yelling 'do I even have to teach you the entirety' so I started moving my head my self and he just yelled 'similarly you bitch, I need to sense your throat' then he commenced to thrust into my mouth, sincerely hard and I should taste salt, it was tough to respire and my jaw ached from being open so extensive and he was, however, using and holding my hair saying 'suck me, quicker, deeper, pass your tongue, quicker'.

I did everything he requested, I so desired to offer him delight but I may want to tell he became respiratory very heavily. I did not need to disappoint him, I grew to become him on now I needed to fulfill him, I closed my eyes and sucked him as speedily as I could seeking to accommodate all of him in my small tight mouth, I in no way slowed, my own pussy was critically aching and throbbing and I wanted to touch it but there was no time, my tongue darted around his lumps and bumps on his penis and my mouth moved his pores and skin up and down and I let it go proper down so I nearly choked on each thrust, my jaw became burning and I failed to stop, up and down, up and down, with a frenzied tempo to fit his continuous thrusting after which the auto stopped.

He advised me to get out and I became shocked, I even though I became doing well for a learner and regarded to be getting very sexy and I was no longer close to domestic. Then I sat up and looked out the windscreen and realized we were on the lake, now not at home. He led me to a picnic desk and lifted me onto it. He told me this is what occurs to little sluts that pervert and he forcibly removed my panties and opened my legs; his fingers grabbed my thighs and absolutely harm the pores and skin as he simply parted my legs wider and wider whilst fucking my pussy along with his finger.

His cock turned into still difficult and putting out of his jeans and earlier than I knew it he was seeking to shove it my vagina where his finger has been in advance. Oh my God, the ache, there has been no manner his cock should ever enter me and he attempted to shove it hurting me and then there has been 'white warm' ache and I knew he had ripped me. He was shoving it inside and out, in and out, real tough and I started crying with ache, however, it also felt properly.

He pulled off my pinnacle and was surprised to peer I had no bra on, he referred to as me a right slut with juicy tits, he grabbed my knockers and squeezed them as he pounded away deep into me, I felt so alive, and when I watched his face he became eyeballing my complete body and grabbing at the whole thing. The picnic desk turned into creating a squeaking noise which was off-setting to him so he carried me still on his cock to the bonnet of the auto and lay on me, still standing and commenced pounding and pounding his cock into me, and telling me to fuck him returned 'move quicker you little bitch''fuck me' it was then I misplaced my inhibitions and grabbed him returned and touched him.

He didn't like it, he instructed me to shut up and fuck him, fuck him difficult, fuck him now, play with your soft massive titties for me, contact his balls - he became giving orders to me to touch the whole thing and I could not cross quick sufficient and my pussy turned into aching with pain, burning. This made him mad and he took his penis out of me, pulled me off the auto bonnet and moved me beside the car with my arms at the roof, a split second later he was entering me from behind, I had by no means heard of it earlier than and my throbbing pussy welcomed it as he touched my knockers madly and reached touched my vagina and clit whilst pumping me from behind - I should infrequently take the pain, the pride, the naughtiness, and without warning this brilliant feeling came proper via my frame lik e a lightning bolt and I writhed and moaned like a whore.

I desired to enjoy the moment as I had never felt it that but MrC pushed me down directly to the floor on my back and climbed on top among my legs - I may want to barely cope with it as everything tingled too much to tolerate but he simply advised me that I had cummed, and I may have to maintain going till he does, because I am a dirty pervert, who likes being fucked, fucked tough and his large cock became my punishment, he thrust so hard it hurt when it something inner, not to mention my whole vagina aching and stretched greater than it has ever been and once I requested to head a little slower.

He laughed and said I shouldn't tease, little bitches get fucked by means of men, it's what you want, and that due to the fact I am younger I should be able to preserve up with him, I could not keep up, he fucked and pounded and his cock were given larger, and I screamed in ache and pleasure and touched his balls which were pounding towards my skin with an exceptional slapping noise, then he pulled his large cock out and frantically wanked it above my stomach - that made me turned on so much and before I knew it liquid was squirting onto my knockers and he was rubbing his squirting cock up my stomach then he put in my mouth and advised me to clean it.

I become so grateful due to the fact I desired to have the feel of it, taste it and do what I could not achieve this nicely earlier, suck him off. He said this was a secret due to the fact others wouldn't recognize and his daughter turned into my best pal and he was right, she wouldn't apprehend. I was so lucky to have been taught via an experienced guy who knows thousands about sex and when I examine older guys my eyes pass directly to their crotch and I want them to control me.

# FUCKED BY MY BEST FRIEND'S DAD

After getting back home from my second 12 months of college I couldn't wait to peer my exceptional pal Jasmine, who I hadn't visible in around six months. Excited to look each different we determined that we would spend the night collectively at her house; talk about university, men, and different lady stuff, watch movies, devour junk food, similar to the coolest ole days. Now I had constantly had a overwhelm on Jasmine's dad, Scott, who became 42, 6'2, muscular, and had quick brown hair and blue eyes that would usually preserve my stare each time we made eye contact. Having no longer seen him in quite a long time, I had forgotten, simply how attracted I became to him, however, that every one modified once I saw him for the first time in over a year, and I knew I had to do what I wished I ought to have usually after I turned into younger. Now this time of the month turned into a horrific time, I became ovulating and I had by no means had sex even as I become, however, I knew that between me being extremely horny from ovulating, a lifelong crush, and staying the night there, there has been no manner I'd have the ability to forestall myself. Luckily Jasmine's mom, Katie, became a nurse, who labored the night shift, so Scott and I would have masses of time without the risk of having his spouse seize us.

Now, once I was given to her residence, we spent some hours in the residing room with Jasmine and her mother and father, watching TV, catching up and talking about our past year at university. Every danger I ought to, I'd flirt a bit with Scott, and lean down exposing any bit of cleavage I could in my white tank pinnacle. Eventually, Katie needed to move to get equipped for work, to have an opportunity to do these more frequently, until shortly after Katie left, at which point, Jasmine and I went as much as her room. We persevered our conversations about the beyond year of university, boys, and our diverse sexcapades, my listing of them being extensively longer than hers. We watched some of our favorite movies, just like we had many times before, but, I had a hard time concentrating on the movie, all I ought to reflect on consideration on changing into her dad. I had continually been too apprehensive to attempt something after I was younger, but now I'd be doing the whole thing I should so as to sleep with him. So, while Jasmine fell asleep on her bed midway through Mean Girls at around 4:00 am I knew this became the perfect time to finally act on what I'd felt for years.

Once I became certain that Jasmine was asleep, I got up off the ground, snuck out of her room and down the hall into her parents' room. I slowly opened the door and peered interior, seeing Scott slumbering on his again. I entered, closed the back door, and immediately took off my black bra and panties. I walked to the end of his bed and pulled the returned cover. Fortunately, he was better able to sleep in a boxer. I grabbed the top of his boxer and pulled down slowly, revealing his cock and ball. I knelt, picked up his soft cock and started slowly and slowly. His cock started to harden and develop in my hand as I picked up the tempo. Once I felt it was tough sufficient I worked his 7 inches long and thick cock into my mouth. Bobbing up and down on his dick slowly, it was given even harder. I took it deeper and deeper whenever I went down, whilst also the usage of my hand to stroke his cock, whilst I sucked it. After a couple of minutes of persistent sucking, I felt Scott jerk awake.

"Katie is that you?" I heard Scott ask in a daze.

"Not precisely," I stated pulling my mouth off his cock. Scott speedily sat up and moved backward, yanking his cock out of my hand.

"Then who the hell are you, and what are you doing?" Scott asked.

"It's Brooke, Mr. Cook," I stated. Scott turned on his bedside lamp and seemed down at me, sporting nothing but my bra and panties.

"What the hell do you observed you are doing Brooke?" Scott Asked as an alternative loudly.

"Shhhh you'll wake up Jasmine, and you recognize exactly what I'm doing," I said before leaning in and kissing him. Our lips met and I kissed him passionately, he did not kiss returned however failed to push me away for some seconds.

"We cannot try this Brooke," Scott said after pushing me away.

"Sure we can, your spouse may not be home for a few hours, and Jasmine is snoozing, we might not get caught," I informed him confidently.

"You positive Jasmine is drowsing?" Scott requested.

"She became out like a light, we've not anything to worry about," I told him.

"Well, in that case..." Scott stated before grabbing me and throwing me up at the bed. He pulled his boxers off and threw them at the ground. I came up to him, grabbed the now somewhat difficult cock, stroked several times and put it in my mouth. I swirled my tongue around the head, and all down his shaft as I took his complete cock in my mouth. I pulled off and gasped for air earlier than Scott grabbed my head and compelled it down on his cock, I gagged as I did not have time to loosen up my throat. He pulled me away and held me down with his cock before passionately kissing me. We kissed deeply for what regarded like minutes earlier than he pulled returned, grabbed my arms and positioned me on my again sideways so that my legs could be free from hitting the bedside. He grabbed my panties and forcibly pulled it down and rancid throwing it apart at the bed, revealing my shaven pussy, whilst I undid my bra, exposing my titties. He squatted on his knees with him eating my pussy like a hungry lion. I let loose a moan the second his tongue made contact with my pussy, my pussy turned into soaking wet and he licked it viciously, he dragged his tongue up and down my sending waves of pleasure through my frame whenever. He hit my clit, which sends a large pulse of satisfaction through me, making me scream a touch. He keeps ravishing my pussy, hitting my clit ever so often, making me moan loudly. Finally, he grew to become his complete interest to my clit, alternating between up and down, and round motions. Knowing precisely what to do subsequent, he began sucking on my clit, which nearly sent me over the edge. As the orgasm approached, my breathing became faster and moaning became more frequent. Sensing this, Scott shoved hands into my pussy at the same time as he continued the onslaught along with his tongue. It didn't take very long after that and I was cumming throughout his fingers and face. I commenced to scream but Scott quickly grabbed my panties and shoved them into my mouth to make me as quiet as possible.

Scott stood up leaned down and kissed me deeply, I may want to taste my pussy juices as we made out passionately. He broke the kiss, grabbed my legs and threw them at the bed with the relaxation of me, still on my again. Then I got on the mattress as well and rubbed the top of his cock against my slit, up and down.

"Please, just shove it in, I want it inside me," I beg and moan. Without announcing a word Scott shoved the complete period of his cock into me forcing me to scream again, as his cock absolutely stuffed me up. He slowly pulled out of me then forcibly shoved it lower back, garnering every other scream from me. He reached down and firmly grasped my titties as he started slowly fucking me. He fucked me with a gradual pace, then every so often, he'd surprise me by violently shoving his cock into me, followed through him returning to the equal tempo as before. I was constantly moaning and every so often screaming from the immense quantity of delight I became receiving. Slowly he started out to pick up the tempo, with the occasional complete thrust, which brought about me to moan and scream louder. At this point, it didn't appear to be counted how loud I turned into Scott didn't appear to care if all and sundry heard, even his daughter, who become simply down the hall. Scott could stop fucking every now and then and bend right down to suck each of my tits, which felt absolutely splendid, him preventing every every so often is what saved him from cumming fast, but it could not delay it forever.

"I'm gonna cum soon Brooke, are you at the pill?" Scott requested through gritted teeth.

"No Pill... And... I am Ovulating," I felt like another orgasmic building so I managed to say.

"Fuuuck!" Was all he  said, as  Scott pushed my  legs lower  back above my head and kicked into overdrive. He pummeled my pussy with the whole thing he had, fucking me harder than he had up to that point. I was moaning and screaming out in satisfaction as I felt his head expand, and his cock twitch, signaling his imminent orgasm. Screaming loudly, Scott stabbed at me with all his might, erupted, and spit out deep into my  defenseless fertile  pussy. I right  now got  here on  his  cock  and screamed out loudly, his cock spurted numerous ropes earlier than he did every other little thrust, making sure he  was as  deep as possible in my pussy, then he collapsed on a pinnacle of me breathing heavily, as his  cock  sprayed  my  pussy  with  its last small  ropes.  I  wrapped my arms around Scott as my orgasm nevertheless rocked my frame. We kissed  passionately  for a  chunk  before he told me  he needed to clean the mattress up   so   his spouse wouldn't discover out.   He climbed off of me and I  was given down, grabbed my garments and left, heading lower back to Jasmine's room.

I   peeked   in   and saw her nonetheless dozing on   her mattress,   so I put my clothes lower back on, went to the identical spot I  was before I left, and fast wiggled deep into sleep, I was exhausted from amazing sex. Jasmine woke  up that morning and apologized for having to hear her dad and mom fucking.

"Yeah, they  have been attempting for another youngster now  that  I'm off   to college,   so they   have been   having intercourse every opportunity they   get, mainly when my mom gets home early   from work, and he or she can get quite loud, so I'm sorry you heard that" Jasmine said clearly apologizing.

"Oh it is no big deal, I nevertheless hear my dad and mom from time to time, so I'm used to it, in any case, I'm starving, let's pass get a few breakfasts," I said status up and heading out her door.

# Me and my Best Friend's Dad

It all began one summertime afternoon. I had clocked 19 at that time and had lived at home even as I had to university and for the reason for this story, so did my quality buddy Tyler. Tyler and I had been friends seeing that third grade and I had gotten to know his family but matters haven't been going that amazing along with his family for some weeks. A few weeks ago, his mum and dad had gotten into a controversy over his dad's work so his dad had moved into an apartment not long ago. His dad (Jason) and his mother have started to get alongside substantially with every other for the reason that then and I assume I heard his dad pronouncing that he turned into trying to move lower back into the house earlier than the summertime had ended. A little bit about me, I had a nice frame too with muscle tissue big enough for me at my age and a nice six-pack. I had continually idea I became straight till a couple of weeks in the past at college that I had my first gay revel in at a party which threw my sexuality off track and I become misplaced and now I'm simply searching for myself.

Well anyways, I was bored one Friday afternoon when I decided to head over to Tyler's house to peer what he was as much as. I had seen Jason's truck out the front of the residence, which had to suggest he turned into over for a visit as usual. After knocking on the front door and getting no response, I began to go home when something had stuck my eye. I remembered that I had seen two guys sucking every different off on the T.V. via the blinds, reflecting off of Jason's rolled up the window. After not knowing what to accept as true with, I crept again up to the window that allows you to see that what I saw become true. There on the T.V. were two dudes bare giving every different head.

I had to see who was watching this so I appeared around the room to discover Jason sitting on the sofa, masturbating to this! I become amazed to what I saw due to the fact I had always an idea that Jason became straight because he changed into married to Tyler's mom.

I also have to say his frame wasn't that bad either. I had never seen Jason naked earlier than and he becomes very attractive! He had some massive muscular tissues and a six-pack considering that he worked out plenty. He additionally had a mild tan and had brief grey hair which I knew was weird due to the fact he became forty-three which seemed like a young age to me and he had short grey whiskers around his mouth and chin. But I say his fine feature became his dick. It had to be as a minimum eleven inches lengthy and it became thick too! Jason was sitting on the sofa, beating his meat furiously at the same time as the men at the T.V. began to fuck each different. After some time had passed, Jason had tilted his head lower back and started to moan and yell in satisfaction. He became yelling and moaning so loud, I may want to hear him through the window.

"AH! Oh yes! YES!! Oh yeah! UGH!! Suck my dick, Clay!" Jason screamed.

I couldn't trust on what I turned into hearing! Jason was fantasizing about me! At that point, I become guessing Jason become about to blow his load due to the fact the guys on T.V. began to cum on every different and he started to tighten up. He started to moan loudly again as he started to cum all over himself. "OH YES! Drink my cum, boy! Drink it all! EAT MY SPERM!!."

After about a minute of this, Jason had released his cock and started to loosen up at the couch along with his eyes closed. A lot of time had to have past when I had got here again to reality. Once I came too, I realized that my cock was looking to develop to complete length in my shorts. I additionally started to end up paranoid, hoping nobody knew I was staring into Tyler's residence so I speedy jumped far from the window and attempted to cover myself until I had reached my residence. Back inside my room, I started to strip down naked and fantasize about this sexy daddy in view that my dad and mom weren't domestic. Only a few matters had run thru my thoughts as I idea about Jason sexually: How large that dick changed into, how badly I desired him, how badly I desired that cock in my mouth and up my ass, and how horrific I desired him to drench me in his jizz. As I jerked off, I knew at that second I desired that dick and I became gonna get it at all cost.

Later that day, I had returned to Tyler's residence however this time, so that it will see Jason, who greeted me on the front door, just wearing shorts and smiling at me.

"Hey buddy, Tyler is not domestic proper now. He, his brother, and his mom all went to Newton Falls for a family reunion and may not be returned for the subsequent three days" Jason defined to me.

I knew this was gonna be my as soon as I a lifetime danger so I had quickly made up a lie so as for me to stay. "That's very well" I began off, "But I become questioning if I ought to live right here with you for the night due to the fact my dad and mom had left to move bail, my sister, out of jail in Columbus and that they locked the door so I cannot get in my house and that is my closing vicinity to go to."

Jason smiled a touch bit bigger. "Sure you may live" he agreed. "Come properly in!."

After Jason had allowed me into the house, he cooked us both dinner and we chilled out in the dwelling room, watching T.V. till it grew dark outside. A wrestling commercial came at the TV which then allowed for the night to start heating up.

"That reminds me" Jason started off speaking to me, "I had seen you and Tyler wrestling the opposite day inside the front yard and also you almost had him. I desired to expose you a few actions so as that will help you pin him fast if you don't thoughts."

"No, I'm cool with it" I responded laid back.

We each got down on the living room floor and we started to wrestle. We did actions repeatedly till I had gotten it down. Everything turned into going top-notch for about a    half-hour till I  felt   a   sharp pain in my right shoulder.

"OUCH!" I yelled barely as I grabbed my shoulder.

"What's wrong" Jason requested a touch worried. "Did I hurt you?"

"No, you did  not." I replied calmly, "It's just my  shoulder. It feels  like it is cramping up or something. Ow..."

"Let  me think" Jason said as  he  reached  over  and gently grabbed  my shoulder, feeling round for the knot. "There it is. Your muscle must have knotted   up.   I   can rub   down it within   the shower along with the hot water beating down on it if you don't mind" he requested me.

"I don't definitely care, I just need for the ache to go away," I said.

And  with  that  note,  Jason advised me to  move to the  toilet with  him. In the  restroom, Jason commenced the bathing water and we each grew to     become away     from each different and     stripped     down. Without searching at one or the other, I hopped into the shower first.

Jason began to  talk to  me  from the  other side of  the  curtain.  "I'll be back in  a  minute,  I  have something to  do  first"  and  with  that, he turned into long gone from the toilet.

Being  alone in  the shower,  I allowed the running water  beat  down  on my shoulder which absolutely felt incredible. a few minutes later, Jason had lower  back and  hopped inside the shower at  the  back  of me.  He grabbed   my   shoulder   and began to rub   down which delivered a few relief and he started out speaking to me.

"So buddy, how have you ever been doing," he asked me.

"I've         been         doing accurate so far,         however, I'm simply careworn right now" I confessed.

"What's been bothering ya?" he requested.

"Well, I feel harassed about my sexuality. I always thought I turned into straight until more than one week in the past at college once I had this experience with this guy. I felt it threw my sexuality off and now I feel stupid for going via this at this age."

"Hey..." Jason said in a caring way "Don't beat yourself up over this. You can be something you need. You can be gay-straight-bi or whatever and do not worry about what humans think of you either. You gotta be you, comply with your coronary heart and also you gotta make yourself happy. We are not here on the way to please others, just stay life anywhere it takes you, and you will be satisfied. I had to examine the equal too lengthy in the past."

I became amazed. "You were stressed about your sexuality too?!" I requested.

"Yes, I was" he replied. "But I know I made the right choice on what I want in this world, and finally it will exercise session for you too."

My shoulder has launched the knot and Jason stopped massaging my shoulder. "There you cross, all better" he informed me happily.

I was so happy with what Jason had instructed me that it felt he started a love fire inside of my coronary heart and I didn't want for it to die out so I had to do something quickly. I pretended to experience light-headed so I fell lower back into Jason's arms, pretending to faint. Jason held me up and spoke to me curiously. "Are you very well?"

"Yeah...I simply feel a bit light-headed is all" I lied.

We then both looked into every other eye and our hearts started to overcome a touch quicker. Jason leaned down and kissed me at the lips. I turned into amazed at the beginning but then I loved it. The kiss turned into passionate however feisty. After we stopped kissing, I could feel his dick beginning to grow and it poked me at the back of the leg. He then appeared down at my nine-inch boner that was growing.

We smiled at each different and I turned off the water. We hopped out of the shower and started to dry off. After a couple of minutes, I felt Jason picking me up and carrying me off to the living room like I became his bride.

In the residing room, Jason had covered the sofa in towels in order that way if we had been wet, we would not destroy the couch. Jason plopped down at the sofa and I was lying in his fingers nonetheless as he grabbed the faraway and placed the homosexual porn that I had seen at the T.V. in advance, back on. It commenced off with the 2 equal dudes sitting on a couch, watching a gay porno of their own as they started to make out. Jason and I checked out every other with an ardor and we began to kiss. Jason had a hold of me with one arm and became transferring his different free hand down my thigh and persevering with down my leg. I had one arm around him and my other loose hand was slowly going over his pecks and gambling with his nipples. We teased every other with tongues and Jason started to rub my nipples along with his thumb as I rubbed his biceps. Jason started to slowly lean me returned and kissed me throughout my neck. Jason started to move slowly downwards on my body. He started to lick and bite my nipples for a few minutes. He endured to move downwards nonetheless and kissed my six-pack while slowly stroking my cock. He sooner or later reached my dick and commenced to go down on me.

He slowly bobbed his head up and down on my dick earlier than taking it lower back out of his mouth and spitting on it. He rubbed the spit all over my cock earlier than slapping it towards his lips and tongue. He positioned my dick back in his mouth and commenced to head a little faster up and down on me. I looked back at the porno and noticed one of the dudes feeding the other dude his dick after which slapping it on his face. Jason started to stroke me again and kiss above my cock and my stomach. He opened huge once more and commenced to suck me off once more. I commenced to fuck his face by forcing my hips up and down. Jason permit me to try to force my cock deep into his throat. Jason stroked me off while kissing my waist and stomach once more. Jason wrapped his fingers around each of my thighs and went all of the way down on my cock, looking to get all of it in without gagging. I placed my hand on the returned of his head and he held himself there for about 20 seconds till he came again up, gasping for breath. He left a little spit trail from my dick to his mouth and then went back down for an excellently longer time.

Jason did this for about 15 minutes, choking on my dick for intervals of time. Each time was longer than the closing. He permits go of my thighs and pulled me closer to him and we commenced to kiss once more.

"How-turned into-that?" Jason requested me in between kisses.

"It become-amazing-have-you-accomplished it-earlier than?" asked in among kissing his lips.

"Oh-yeah-I-had practice-before. Sometimes-with-buddies-at-their houses-or-sometimes-when-Tyler-and-his-mom-were-gone, I-would-cross-down-on-Rodney-all-the-time" he defined.

We stopped kissing as I checked out him amazed again. "You had homosexual intercourse with Rodney?" I asked.

"Yeah all the time whilst Tyler and his mother had been gone or I could whenever I and him went out somewhere. He became continually death to get his hands on his daddy's dick" Jason defined.

I become puzzled in these new records when Jason got off of the sofa and on the ground in front of me, looking for me to enroll in him at the ground. I got up too and sat down with Jason and he began to give an explanation for me what he desired to do next.

"Okay, Clay. Do you understand a way to 69?" he requested.

"Well yeah!" I stated with an excited smile.

"Good" Jason stated smiling back at me and he had me lay down on my back. He was given on top of me and exposed his hollow for me to the rim. He sat on his knees so he would not overwhelm my chest after which he lifted my legs into the air. I started to rim his ass as he slowly stroked and teased my cock. I stuck my tongue into his hole several time and I started to finger him. He set free little moans letting me know I was doing an awesome activity for it being my first time. After a couple of minutes, he started to reward me by sucking my dick once more. He was given even more snug through putting my legs at the back of his arms and he commenced to play with my hollow and he started to spank me lightly. He grabbed my ass tightly and fingered my entire with one hand, spanked my other cheek lightly along with his different hand, and persevered to blow me along with his mouth, all in one! I commenced feeling like he needed a few greater treats for giving me so a great deal satisfaction so I started to tease his cock with my arms at the same time as I stilled rimmed and fingered him. After a couple of minutes, he lifted his again quit to place his dick in my face and I began to blow him. His cock was so huge and I tried my high-quality to fit all of him that I may want to in my mouth.

His dick was too big that allows you to be right above my head so it went a little down my neck as I licked his shaft up and down. I needed to do my high-quality to get that dick all the way down my throat so I inhaled all that I could and took him all in until I touched his balls with my nostrils. I wiggled it around in my mouth, trying not to gag and trying to preserve myself there for so long as I should. Jason commenced to moan louder and a touch quicker, which allowed for me to recognize I was giving him the works. I at the end needed to let myself breathe so I took his dick out of my mouth and I coughed over and over, trying to inhale all the sparkling air I could.

"If you don't experience which you cannot get it all in your mouth, I would not advise that you attempt to take me all in" Jason informed me. "Just absorb as lots as you can."

And with that, he went back to rimming my ass. I had to please Jason all I ought to so I took him all in again, as much as his balls and I began to play with his hollow once more. He commenced to moan even louder than remaining time and I took him out of my mouth, seeking to breathe again. He lifted himself on all fours and turned himself around till his dick became going through me.

"Let me assist you to breathe if you want me all the manner on your mouth," he said.

Jason lifted my legs inside the air and began to provide an explanation for me what to do.

"First, relax," he started to explain, "You can get more in case you chill out. Breathe via your nose for air when you want it. Don't try and take me in all of the way before everything. Just get in as a lot as you could and then try to take more of my cock on your mouth inch by way of an inch. And finally, if you experience like which you want to get your mind off of gagging, hum. It's pretty hard to hum and gag on equal time."

I obeyed what Jason wanted me to do and he slowly inserted his cock into my mouth. He had to at least be five inches in when I should sense him behind my throat. I started to breathe in and out via my nostrils while slowly seeking to get 6 inches in my mouth. After some time, I got to 8 inches in my mouth and Jason was playing it. He had tilted his head lower back and commenced to moan softly even as maintaining my legs up. Eventually, I got all 11 inches in my mouth and Jason was in heaven even as I persevered to try my exceptional to loosen up.

"That a boy, Clay," Jason said softly. "Oh, suck my dick. Suck it. Your gonna get a large hot reward in a while on your golden mouth."

Jason started to stroke me off too however slowly so I could keep my cum. Jason took his dick out of my mouth and seemed down at me whilst he slapped it towards my face. His dick became so big it reached the top of my head. He then stood up and I got on my knees as I went back down on him with something came up. I had gotten Jason halfway down my throat while he got stuck. I commenced to panic a bit while he tried to calm me down.

"Oh, a susceptible spot," he said with a grin. "It's OK. Clay, just open extensive and I'll do the relaxation."

I opened my mouth as wide as I should get it and Jason pulled out his dick, and I ought to breathe once more.

"This passed off some times before with my wife and Rodney. They weren't cautious enough to live extensive open and they got my cock caught of their throats. It's clean to pull right out once they open all of the way again however I want to have fun with it" Jason teased. "You better inhale all the air you can and open up again."

I inhaled as a good deal air as I could and opened up my mouth as wide as my jaws could allow me. Jason inserted most of his cock into my throat once more and was given caught as soon as extra. Jason grabbed the back of my head one greater and pushed his cock all the way down until my lips have been touching his pubes. He regarded down into my eyes that started to water with his pleasured face and moved my head from side to side speedy, despite the fact that he becomes caught. He tapped the back of my head, which I knew turned into the signal with a view to open extensive again and he pulled himself out, leaving me to gasp for air and allow for the tears to roll down my cheeks. I wiped the tears away and appeared back up at Jason again as he held his dick and instructed me to open once more. I opened extensive again and Jason shoved himself returned in once more and glued himself as soon as greater. I started to rip up once more and looking at Jason, he left himself in his mouth as he talked to satisfy sweetly.

"You're a good boy, Clay. You should get my dick as a treat. Don't cry" Jason stated as he wiped my tears away. "You'll get it in your ass quickly sufficient."

I felt like I turned into gonna bypass out but at the ultimate moment, Jason pulled himself out and I began to fill my lungs with fresh air again. This went on like this for about a half of hour. Jason would insert himself, have a touch a laugh with me and sweet communicate before pulling himself out and I regained air again.

Jason sooner or later stopped and helped me up off of my knees.

"Sorry I held my dick for your throat for so long, I just wanted that identical pride once more" he apologized.

Jason then became towards me and hugged me tight to allow for me to recognize he wasn't seeking to be cruel. It becomes ok for me and quickly sufficient he had me through the hand, taking me upstairs. We got to the master bedroom and he started to kiss me passionately earlier than pushing me back at the mattress. He was given on the bed to, on his knees in front of me so we had been at the equal eye level, and he commenced to kiss me again. He stopped shortly after to provide an explanation to me about what was gonna take place subsequently.

"You did so well for permitting me to have my satisfaction, you're going to get the quality rimjob of your life! Turn around and on all four" he ordered.

I did what he advised me to do being so thrilled about what was gonna appear next. Jason spread my cheeks open with his palms and started to rim my ass like never earlier than. He poked his tongue at my entire and began to lick it up and down earlier than beginning it a little and sticking his tongue internal. He spit on my hole after which licked it up. He licked and played with my balls and began to tease my dick together with his tongue at the same time as he was at it. Jason began to speedy flavor my dick and then lick my ass and repeated that for a couple of minutes. After that, he took each one in every of my nuts into his mouth and massaged them too. He becomes licking my dick and commenced to spit all over my hole before licking it all up. He speedy ran his tongue backward and forward all over my hole after which caught his tongue back inner me. He commenced to tease my ass with licks and then he started to finger me. First, it was with one finger, then two hands, then three palms, and then 4 arms. He was about to suit his whole hand in my ass once I could not take the irresistible satisfaction anymore.

"Jason, please! I need you to fuck my ass with your massive cock! Fill my hole up with it! Rip my ass apart! Make me experience you all night if I must to be able to get that warm cum!" I had begged him.

"I concept you would never ask!" he stated sexually.

He stopped rimming me and grabbed my ass several instances. He left the room for a second and returned with a few lubrication. He put the lube throughout his dick and then started to slowly insert himself inner me. It began to hurt before everything so I had requested for him to stop.

"Relax your ass, Clay. I'll stop pushing till you sense ready to continue" he stated lightly.

It turned into about five minutes till he becomes geared up and back at it once more. He slowly pushed himself slowly into me till he was all of the way in. My ass became on fire but additionally filled with satisfaction. Jason slowly pulled out, being cautious with me until his penis head become nonetheless left internal. He started to insert himself once more a little faster than the closing time and then back out until his tip was left inside me. This happened for about some other short time and then the pain had left me. Jason had commenced to choose up the tempo and in no time, he had a hold on me by using my hips and was fucking me swiftly. After some time, Jason got off the mattress, still internal me and pulled me off the bed till my dick became squished in opposition to the facet of it. Jason got on his knees at the ground and persevered to fuck me like that for another 15 minutes. I was in so an awful lot of pleasure and I had to hang onto the bed for support.

"Oh, Jason!" I moaned, "Your dick is so large."

Jason picked me up and laid me on the table on my side and started fucking me hard. Shortly after, I was on my back, on the ground with my legs in the air, him plundering my ass still. Eventually, he had me back at the mattress, dealing with far away from him while he fucked me. In the very last position, Jason had me sitting on his lap, nevertheless protecting me via my hips and we kissed earlier than he drilled me. I was bouncing up and down on him as I become in a massage chair. We have been each moaning so loudly no marvel the neighbors did not hear us.

After an extended time, Jason had stopped drilling me and had me get off of his lap. He had me sit down on my knees, at the ground even as he left for the bathroom to wash the smell of ass off of his dick. He again rapidly, jerking himself off furiously and got here over to my face.

"Open wide Clay, I've been watching for this second for a whilst" Jason stated.

I opened my mouth and started to suck his dick again and matched the rate of his hand. I kept bobbing my head up and down while Jason started to moan loudly like how he did earlier that day.

"AH! Oh yes! YES!! Oh yeah! UGH!! Suck my dick, Clay! AHHHHHH-" Jason yelled.

At that second, Jason's dick erupted with hot, sticky cum and it filled my mouth speedy. I tried my quality to swallow it all but I had permit lots escape my mouth and subsequently took his dick out of my mouth and jacked him off extra, to permit for the cum to keep flowing. Jason shot several hundreds of cum before finishing it and I had sucked his dick smooth of any get admission to cum. A lot had gone down my throat and plenty greater was on my face. Jason had his palms on his hips, trying to seize his breath as he appeared down at me and smiled with joy. He got down on his knees too and lick my face smooth of cum. Jason then had me rise and moved me to the wall. Jason started to suck my dick furiously whilst he had both of his hands on my ass cheeks, fingering my hollow again. He might maintain sucking speedy, stop to stroke me a bit, and then suck me off again. I slowly slid down the wall if you want to sit and Jason persisted to blow me while fingering my ass.

I started to moan to make Jason know I was beginning to get close. He seemed up at me as he took my dick out of his mouth and started to conquer it again his lips earlier than going lower back to sucking it. Jason began to finger me tightly once more and my frame started to tighten up. Jason knew it was coming quick so he had me arise even as he becomes still sucking and fingering me and started to bob his head speedy up and down my shaft. I commenced to moan like loopy after which started to yell.

"I'm cumming! I'm cumming! Jason, I'm cumming!" I yelled.

Jason shoved one finger deep into my hand and held it there as he went all the way down on me. I started to shot my load all in his mouth and he started to swallow it. He jerked me off whilst smiling at me and let his tongue trap all the tongue flying out of my dick. I ultimately finished shooting my load whilst Jason had stuck nearly all of my cum. He had a few left in his whiskers after which took his finger out of my ass. I lick his face easy of the remaining jizz and then we both plopped down at the bed, seeking to capture our breath.

I felt awful about mendacity to Jason earlier so I decided I wanted to come clean with him.

"Hey Jason, there's something I need to inform you..." I began off.

"Your dad and mom have been in reality home this whole time," he said at the start together with his eyes closed and then looking over at me with a smirk.

"Yeah" I spoke back pressured as soon as extra. "But how did you-"

"I saw them leave after which come lower back to the store after you got here over" he interrupted me.

Jason smiled at me and I felt a touch embarrassed.

"Oh, and subsequent time you spot me jack-off, why don't you come in and be a part of me" he informed me at the same time as nevertheless smiling, knowing I was looking him the complete time.

I was surprised again about how he knew all of this but I just stopped trying to placed it all collectively and cuddled as much as him in mattress. He held me close and we kissed each different again before he explained one final issue to me.

"One final issue Clay" Jason commenced off.

"What is it this time?" I stated with a smile.

"Tyler, Rodney, and their mother might not be back for another three days..." Jason informed me.

"I surprise what we will do inside the meantime," I said, finishing his sentence with a laugh.

"It will be the excellent time of your life" Jason guaranteed. "Goodnight Clay."

Jason kissed me goodnight after which held me near as I drifted off to sleep, considering the start of a new relationship.

# TEENAGER'S ASS

Darren Lyons was quite amazed whilst he responded to his doorbell and beheld Jennifer, a friend of his daughter there. The younger girls had graduated from excessive school collectively and were currently in their 2nd year at a local community college, so the traveler has acknowledged her pal might not be home.

"Hi, Jennifer," he greeted her. "Stephanie's in magnificence, where I might anticipate you to be this hour of day."

"I understand that, Darren. I reduce class to come and see you. Can I come in?"

"Of path." He stepped apart to let the quite youngster enter.

Being outgoing and now not liking formality, Darren became on first-name phrases with most of his daughter's buddies, which includes Jennifer. She had been in the residence typically, and headed immediately to the own family room, in which she sat on the sofa and smiled up at him. He had accompanied without delay in the back of her, admiring her very shapely ass encased in tight blue denims. Jennifer's breasts had been very appealing too and, from the way they have been swaying when she walked past Darren, they had been manifestly unfettered by way of a bra, underneath the crimson t-shirt she wore. Her face changed into quite too, with green eyes, a lovable snub nose, and a peaches-and-cream complexion crowned by means of tender, curly auburn hair that fell to her shoulders.

He sat at the sofa too, now not so near as to seem aggressive however no longer a long way enough away to be standoffish. "What's in your thoughts, Jen?"

She regarded unable to solution right away, which was ordinary, because on no account was she bashful. Finally, she managed. "Darren, do you have got an amazing sex life?"

That become an unexpected question, coming from female or lady as younger as Jennifer, but he spoke back it as pleasant he should. "It's okay, even though no longer as properly because it was with my wife before she died. Could be better, I suppose, but I'm no longer complaining. I hope you're now not going to get into specifics, even though, because a gentleman in no way kisses and tells."

"I'm glad to hear that ultimate component, due to the fact that I'm curious about something, and I wouldn't need absolutely everyone to realize about it. Not even Steph."

"Especially not Stephanie."

Jennifer persisted. "If I asked you to do something, could you think it becomes crazy or incorrect?"

Darren preferred the manner the conversation was going. He did not regard the buddies of his daughter as sex objects, despite the fact that some of them, in particular Jennifer, were pretty attractive and sexy. He could by no means try to make a pass at one in every of them, however he could additionally in no way refuse a sexual overture from a quite woman, even one as younger because the cutie-pie subsequent to him at the couch. Wanting to encourage the route the communication became going, he responded carefully.

"Jennifer, if two adults have sexual amusing collectively and they revel in it and nobody receives harm, there's nothing crazy or wrong with it."

"Well, that's what I say too. There's some thing I want to find out about, but now not with my boyfriend. I'd be afraid he could inform the other guys, and I don't need a popularity as a freak. That's why I want to do some thing with somebody like you, who may not blab to everyone about it. Are you willing to do it with me? If we do, will you promise now not to tell every body, no longer even your daughter?"

"As long as nobody receives harm, sure. What is it you want to do?"

Until that time, they were facing every other however, whilst Jennifer answered that question, she became her face away and mumbled "I want you to screw me within the butt."

Darren wasn't sure he understood what had simply been said. "In the butt? You want me to screw you within the butt?"

Jennifer raised her face and said, a whole lot more clearly "Yes. I want you to screw me in the butt. But I do not need you to inform anyone. Will you do it? Have you ever carried out it earlier than?"

"Yes. That's yes, I have, however now not for a long term, and sure, I will, if you really need me to."

"Yes, I sincerely do. Can we do it here at the davenport?"

"We may want to, but upstairs in my bed might be higher."

"Okay, permit's pass upstairs and do it. Did it harm the alternative girl? The one you probably did it with before?"

"No, it failed to hurt her and it won't hurt you both, except a bit bit at first. We'll ought to be cautious to make certain it doesn't, however I'll inform you about that when we start."

Darren rose from the couch and supplied his hand to the younger woman who might be doing some thing with him he hadn't completed on the grounds that earlier than he were given married. His overdue wife had been fairly broad-minded about intercourse but, the one time he had stated anything about the possibility, she had replied through pronouncing the idea grossed her out. He and Jennifer walked arm in arm up the stairs and down the short hallway to his bedroom.

There become a small second of embarrassment to Darren because he hadn't made his mattress that day, and the room turned into in any other case untidy, but Jennifer did not appear to observe. She walked over to the mattress and leaned on it, as though she was checking out the mattress, and straightened up, a nervous smile on her face. He concept she could have been having 2d mind, however he was incorrect. The younger woman had steeled herself in advance to make the request, and turned into now not going to returned out.

"What will we do first?"

Darren wasn't going to back out either. He have been deliberating what a surely appropriate ass she had, and every other possibility had happened to him. Fucking her lovely ass was something he very much wanted to do, but it wasn't the best component he appreciated to do with anyone like Jennifer.

"Are you fearful?" he requested her. "It's perfectly ordinary to be a piece tense."

"I am a touch, questioning what it'll experience like. I wish it does not harm."

"Like I stated, it will, however only a little bit and just for a little whilst. But in case you are apprehensive, I recognise how that will help you loosen up."

"How?"

"If I eat your pussy till you climax, it will loosen up you loads. And if you are precise and comfortable, it won't hurt at all."

"Would you be inclined to try this for me too?"

"I'll be satisfied to. I imply, I'll without a doubt enjoy doing it."

Darren stepped forward and took preserve of the hem of Jennifer's t-shirt and began to pull up on it. She raised her palms and he carefully tugged it up past her breasts and off over her head and tossed it onto a corner of the mattress. Jen shook her hair back into area, making her small but shapely breasts sway and bounce, and making Darren nearly drool on the sight. She loosened the waist of her blue denims, driven them down round her ass and hips and sat on the mattress to allow Darren to drag them the rest of the way off. With superb alacrity, he did, after removing her shoes and sox and piling all her clothing together. That left the young splendor carrying simplest her striped bikini panties, however she failed to appear embarrassed over her near nudity.

Wanting to get everything organized earlier and to do it proper, Darren placed a easy case on the pillow she could be using and went to fetch a bottle of baby oil and a humid towel from the bathroom. The oil had been there for over a 12 months, but ought to nevertheless suffice as a lubricant. While he become long gone, Jennifer lay supine on the mattress, her head nestled inside the pillow, and waited to be organized for her experimentation in anal sex. She loved receiving oral sex from boys and guys too, and considered Darren's offer to be some thing of a bonus.

He idea of it almost the same manner, except as an advantage for him, and he knelt beside her and lightly cupped her nearest breast in his hand. It turned into corporation, with warm, clean pores and skin, and felt exact in his hand, however her nipple felt better to his tongue when he leaned ahead and started licking it. It felt top to Jennifer too, and he or she started out cooing happily, particularly when the man pleasuring her began dividing his attentions between the two sweet, red nubbins.

"Mmmm, Darren, that feels simply desirable," she murmured, and the squirming of her frame emphasized what she said.

"It feels excellent to me too," he replied but, after that, his mouth became too busy with greater exciting sports for him to do any greater talking.

Jennifer had no criticism about the lack of communique, due to the fact what he turned into doing felt notable to her. The man whose mattress she was sharing became no longer the first man or woman to fondle her nipples with his tongue, but he appeared to enjoy it an awful lot more than any of her boy pals ever had. The sensations have become even better while Darren drew one among her very sensitive breasts into his mouth and commenced sucking, whilst his tongue persisted caressing her nipple and areola. Once once more, he alternated between the adorable globes. She felt a connection hooked up among them and her clit, and Jennifer knew her pussy become starting to produce the fragrant juices she knew might trap him to lick her decrease on her body.

He smelled the delightful aroma too, and Darren smiled to himself at how the lady in his bed was so responsive and what an exceptional time she was having, which gave him a exceptional time too. He started out licking and nuzzling and kissing his manner down her slim frame, starting with the musky channel among the succulent twins which had felt so extraordinary in his mouth. That became exactly what Jennifer wanted too, and she driven gently on his shoulders to propel him greater quick to his goal.

When his mouth reached the elastic waistband of her bikini panties, Darren raised his head and grinned on the delectable aroma and the spreading stain within the crotch. He slid away from bed and fast were given lower back on at the foot, walked on his knees until he become among Jennifer's legs and reached out to insert his fingertips in that waistband. When she raised her ass away from bed, he pulled her panties down in order that they slipped around her adorable ass, down her thighs and all of the manner off, leaving the teenager bare in front of him. She raised her legs and, when he ducked underneath, let them relaxation on his shoulders. Darren wrapped his hands across the thighs framing his face and leaned in more closely, leaving his face inches from the beautiful pussy his tongue became about to start sharing delight with.

And, it turned into surely a factor of beauty. Jennifer did not shave herself there, and had no want to accomplish that, due to the fact her sparse pubic hair, the identical quite auburn color as that on her head, did nothing to hide her creamy pores and skin. Darren saw how, from her arousal, her swollen inner lips had been blossoming through her slit and, whilst he lightly spread the edges, he became treated to a super fragrant cloud that arose from the pinkness. Small drops of her clean juices, the source of the pleasing scent, adhered to her lips and, while he licked them off, their taste was even greater delicious than their aroma. Avidly, he started searching out more of the nectar anyplace it had spattered.

He started with the smooth, smooth pores and skin at the insides of her thighs, sluicing up all the juices along with his tongue, and persevered to her crotch, in which he caught a few that had been dripping freshly from the red hole that was their supply. The texture of her easy skin underneath his tongue turned into the maximum pleasant sensation of the sensuous pleasures he was receiving. After swallowing the hottest of her nectar, Darren began licking one of Jennifer's outdoor lips. As he were sure it would be, her pubic hair became so tender and downy, it felt as top to his tongue as her bare pores and skin had, and his eager mouth meandered all the manner to Jennifer's Mount of Venus. He kissed her there and raised his face to peer her reactions to what he turned into doing.

They have been even better than he had predicted. Her eyes had been closed in bliss, and her mouth turned into partly open, whilst her head was tossing from side to side on the pillow. The teen's frame became writhing beneath him, and he knew her pussy would soon begin fucking up into his face. Darren grinned, but best briefly, due to the fact his mouth had much higher things to do, and he brought it backpedal to wherein he had commenced and devoured all of the scrumptious juices Jennifer's pussy had simply provided for him.

Her pal's father become a long way from being the first guy to eat the young lady's pussy. Any boy or guy who wanted to be her boyfriend needed to please her that manner, or he ought to forget about any intimate relationship. She cherished having a mouth caressing her lips and clit, and they continually added her to a climax, but the guy whose face became shifting about among her thighs become something in reality special, even for her. He had spent extra time on her breasts than every person else ever had, and he or she cherished each 2d of it and each stroke of his tongue, and he had transferred his attentions to her pussy at precisely the right time. Now, she may want to feel repeated waves of bliss washing over her body everywhere his mouth traveled.

She favored watching him too, and her eyes have been slitted, no longer closed, so she noticed Darren's face seem and kiss her mons before disappearing. She felt him lick all around her love hole and begin up on her other outer lip. It felt so appropriate, and had because he started, her body become bouncing everywhere in the bed, and the quite younger girl started thrusting her pussy against his face. She believed in letting go and reveling within the sexual ministrations of her partner, so all her erotic moves were natural and involuntary. She saw his face upward thrust above her mons again, and this time she smiled and interrupted her completely satisfied cooing to encourage him in what he become doing.

"Oh, Darren, it really is even better. I've never felt some thing as fab as what you're doing to me."

"I'm satisfied you like it, due to the fact I do too. You positive have a lovely pussy."

He could have said more, but he turned into much more interested by persevering with to consume that stunning pussy. Darren should smell the aroma of a large quantity of clean juices, and he knew they would be scrumptious, and he desired to reach them quickly and consume them while they had been at their most up to date. After he did, licking Jennifer's pussy clean of all of the nectar, his tongue began caress her between a couple of internal and outer lips.

He began with the small, ultra-clean vicinity between the origins of the labia and licked slowly upward. When he reached the point in which the two lips were close collectively, Darren tilted his head slightly, so he may want to slide his tongue into the seam and caress both of them at once. The outer turned into slick and easy with her scrumptious juices and the internal lip became puffy with her arousal and felt like a warm colourful sponge under his tongue. He licked upward until he reached the vicinity wherein the internal lip ends and combines with Jennifer's other inner lip to shape her clit hood.

Darren raised his head once more and smiled at the sight of the treasured morsel it need to had been protecting, which become so swollen it had pushed the hood out of the manner. It resembled a lovely pink pearl. He additionally smiled on the sight of Jennifer, whose body was tossing and bucking all over the mattress, a lot that he had to dangle tightly to her thighs to maintain her from throwing them both onto the floor. Darren failed to appearance very long, due to the fact he a good deal desired to delicately stroke his tongue across the pinnacle of the clit hood, which produced another spurt of her juices.

Her pussy were eaten several times earlier than, however Jennifer had in no way gotten a lot satisfaction as she was that day. She typically had an orgasm, despite the fact that a number of her boyfriends thought of that climax as something to rush through to be able to get to the fucking, but her friend's father become taking a long time bringing about that climactic moment. She knew it might be one in all the maximum momentous of her life. His tongue on her clit had simply come near igniting the explosion that might be her orgasm, however his mouth went from there returned to in which he had started, and she or he felt him licking some more of her body's maximum sensitive places. She should experience herself thrashing all around the bed and hear her moans of bliss that have been beginning to result in whimpers and become, in general, getting some of the best sexual satisfaction she had ever recognised.

Darren became having a splendid time too, easily the great when you consider that earlier than his spouse died inside the automobile accident. Jennifer turned into genuinely a hotsy, who in reality knew what she favored and wasn't afraid to demonstrate her satisfaction while she were given it. Like maximum men who like to consume pussy, a major part of the pleasure derived is having the girl immensely enjoy what is taking place and to allow him understand it, both verbally or through her movements. Besides having what just could have been the most delectable pussy he had ever eaten, the lady below his mouth became doing all he ought to have requested for in that regard.

Her actions became even wilder while he commenced licking her other pair of inner and outer lips the identical way as he had completed to the primary. Jennifer's pussy become jamming so difficult in opposition to his mouth, it felt as though she was trying to wrap it round his face. Her legs had been thrusting out and returned over his shoulders like a hard and fast of pistons, and her moans of bliss were finishing in whimpers. By the time his mouth sooner or later reached her clit again, he knew she became as aroused as she might get, and it was time to engulf the precious morsel and suck and lick it until she climaxed.

"Uh! Uh! Uh!" Jennifer whimpered, as she thrashed everywhere in the bed. "Oh, god! Suck my clit!" she advised Darren when his face seemed once more.

She failed to realize if it became due to her urging or not, however she saw his head flow forward and felt his mouth wrap around her clit and start sucking, and she realized his tongue became caressing her there too. "Yes! Yes!" she cried. "Suck me proper there." As wild as her movements have been, they became even extra erratic as his tongue and lips endured doing what she wanted, till she felt her body start to explode.

"Oh, god!" she howled ecstatically, and all her movements after that were reflexive.

Jennifer's thighs clamped tightly across the face of the man who had brought her to that fabulous condition, and her fingers grabbed the again of his head pressing his face against her pussy, which persisted ramming against his mouth. She sang out loudly of her delight, while bouncing up and down on the bed, swinging her legs wildly backward and forward. Darren clung to the wild young lady's legs and stored his mouth clamped round her clit and continued with the sucking and licking.

When she climaxed, all of Jennifer's muscular tissues clenched and she plastered her pussy in opposition to his face for a very last time. After her super orgasm, Jennifer collapsed returned onto the bed along with her palms sprawled out at her sides. Her legs launched their grip, however remained draped over Darren's shoulders. He moved returned slightly, and pressed his face tightly against her pussy again to ceremonial dinner on the wealth of nectar that had been produced. He licked it from her thighs, her crotch and anywhere it had spattered, even sucking it from the lovable red region that had secreted it. When he become done, Darren moved lower back from her frame and off the bed to visit the nightstand for the infant oil, towel and condom he could need to do what Jennifer had come to him to invite for.

When he returned to the mattress, he sat down to take away his pants and undies so he become as bare because the girl whose ass he could be fucking. His cock become as difficult and ready because it had ever been, and he effortlessly rolled the condom into vicinity. Jennifer have been mendacity on her lower back with her eyes closed and a massive smile on her face while he had gotten off the bed, and he or she was still smiling just as broadly. Her eyes were open, although, and her smile grew even wider when she noticed his cock all prepared to serve her.

"That become awesome, Darren. I don't suppose I've ever cum so huge-time before."

"I'm happy, as it was fantastic for me too. I truely loved having you cum like that. I desire you are ready and proper and comfortable, due to the fact it's time for us to do the experiment you got here here for."

"I'm prepared. Just tell me what to do."

"First, take that other pillow and roll over onto your front along with your legs huge apart and slip it below your stomach." When she had complied, he persisted. "Reach returned and unfold your ass cheeks so I can get you greased up." When she become equipped for him to do what turned into needed, he knelt among her legs.

After admiring Jennifer's shapely naked ass, Darren opened the bottle and reached between her smooth cheeks to apply the thumb and hands of 1 hand to pry open her lovable purple rosebud. He located the open top of the bottle towards the tiny hole they had been growing and squeezed in a huge dollop of the infant oil. Preferring to apply greater than sufficient than much less, specifically given that it might be her first time, he squeezed in another gush and replaced the cap at the bottle.

"Oooo, that feels appropriate," she murmured.

Darren smiled at her response, because he knew it'd soon experience even better. He cautiously inserted, all of the manner to his knuckle, the center finger of the hand he had used to open her ass and unfold the lube evenly. Jennifer cooed her satisfaction again, and her shapely ass began squirming. It become apparent to him she would absolutely love being fucked there, and he knew he could enjoy it just as a good deal. When he eliminated his finger from the younger female,

Darren implemented the leftover infant oil to his latex-covered cock and wiped his fingers on the towel.

"Keep maintaining yourself open," he advised her, and leaned ahead, one hand on the mattress beside Jennifer and the alternative guiding his cock.

After Daren felt the top make touch, he moved it up and down and to and fro to be sure the lubrication became nicely-unfold. When he was sure it was, he gave a firm thrust forward, and felt the give up of his cock wedge into the tight hollow being held open for him.

"Oh!" Jennifer grunted, and he or she seemed to move ahead away from the stiff intruder.

"Did that hurt?"

"No. Yes, only a little at first, however it feels properly now. Mmmm, truly, properly.""That's proper." Darren smiled on the response, which became the expected one, and thrust ahead once more, driving an inch of his tough shaft into the tight hollow.

"Ooo, yeah," Jennifer murmured. "That feels virtually desirable now."

"That's good; just live relaxed, and I'll take my time. If it starts offevolved to hurt, let me know, and I'll stop."

"Oh, don't prevent. It maintains getting better and higher."

Darren squeezed his finger into the tight hollow beside his cock and moved it all of the way around to search for any loose skin or other ability problem. Finding none, he thrust ahead again, and every other inch of his cock burrowed into the tight region where it was being made so welcome. Jennifer expressed her joy with the new enjoy and urged him to keep, which he did so gladly. His cock turned into deep sufficient inner her that he now not needed to guide it, so he located both palms on her hips, for leverage and because he preferred the feel of her smooth skin. He pulled lower back against her and thrust forward once more, and maximum of the rest of his cock plowed into the hot ass. Darren lay on top of the younger female for about a minute, letting pride throb from his cock buried in the tight hollow underneath him.

She had by no means felt something like what was taking place, and Jennifer could sense herself squirming at the bed and pay attention herself cooing in delight. The big cock imbedded in her ass dispatched waves of total joy through her frame, as it stretched her greater than she might have believed possible. Her erratic actions jerked the huge giver of pleasure round in her ass and, the extra it moved interior her, the higher it felt. When the person above her commenced slowly drawing it returned, she felt a small twinge of loss.

It failed to final long, although, and his cock surged lower back interior her, stretching her ass and adjacent channel anew, and sending new and even extra powerful currents of joy through her. It penetrated even greater deeply than it have been, and she could even experience Darren's pubic hair tickling the insides of her cheeks. Jennifer was moaning in bliss from what his cock was doing for her, and he pulled it maximum of the manner our and rammed it back into her once more. This time, she was so eager for the amazing erotic satisfaction, she did her satisfactory to fuck back to fulfill it, till her body and his got here firmly collectively.

Darren saw what she was doing, besides feeling her frame shifting, and made a suggestion. "Do you need to get on your knees? You can be plenty more lively that manner."

This made feel to Jennifer. "Good concept. Help me get up."

He drove his shaft all of the way into her and pulled returned on her hips at the same time as she driven up towards the mattress. They ended up with him kneeling at the back of her, along with his cock imbedded in her ass and his palms resting on her hips. They stayed like that for a few seconds, before Darren drew most of the way out, paused with simply the head nonetheless internal, and drove slowly ahead. Jennifer pushed again against the bed to meet him and the result turned into his hips squashed against her tender ass cheeks and his cock even in addition inner her.

To Jennifer, the feeling turned into even more splendid than the pride she had gotten whilst lying face down. To make it better, she bowed her again to present a better goal and to take Darren's cock any other fraction of an inch more deeply into her ass. She even pressed her face towards the pillow she held in her hands, partly muffling her moans of bliss at the same time as pushing returned together with her elbows to meet every stroke he made.

And there have been a lot of them, due to the fact Darren plunged his cock time and again into the very inviting ass before him. Jennifer's frame turned into swaying backward and forward, and her hips were swiveling, riding her knees into the mattress. She knew her orgasm was imminent, and reached up among her thighs to try to play along with her clit. Once once more, Darren noticed what she was looking to do and, with the way her frame become weaving from left to proper and up and down, he feared she might lose her balance and topple over, so he made a suggestion.

"Let me do that, Jennifer. I can reach your pussy better from right here. Just preserve shifting like you've got been, and you will cum like mad again."

That was what she desired and anticipated, so the auburn-haired beauty put both her arms lower back on the bed and concentrated on completely giving herself over to the top notch satisfaction she was getting. Darren reached round – now not with the hand that had been in her ass - to her pussy however, before starting to fondle her clit, he scraped up as tons of the nectar as he ought to and licked it from his fingers and hand, relishing its flavor again. When he had eaten as lots as he could collect, he located the swollen morsel that he sought and, along with his thumb and forefinger, lightly squeezed it among two folds of her internal lips.

"Yes! Yes! Right there," Jennifer exhorted him. "Play with me there and make me cum!"

Darren absolutely needed no urging. He was also prepared to cum from the teenager's tight ass squeezing and liberating his shaft, however he wanted her to climax first. He started stroking her clit within the identical pace as he become driving his cock inside and outside of Jennifer's ass.

"Harder! Faster!" She pled with him. "Give it to me quicker. I want to cum!"

He did what she desired. Darren started fucking tougher and faster, ramming his cock into Jennifer's tight, oily ass, and she matched his extended speed. Abruptly, she cried out joyfully that she become cumming.

Her moves have been developing wilder, and they became more erratic than that they had already been, her torso was tossing up and down, and she or he might have virtually fallen if Darren hadn't been gripping her hips. He persevered plunging his cock inside and outside of her ass, until she cried out once more, incoherently however even more ecstatically. All Jennifer's muscle tissue clenched; she rammed her ass back against his cock for a final time and started out to sag ahead.

Darren permitted her to fall slowly, maintaining his cock in her ass, till Jennifer become lying full length below him. He resumed driving his cock in and until his very own climax exploded, and he shot a gush of cum into his condom, but he failed to forestall right away. Instead, he saved fucking her for almost another minute, till he had ejaculated twice greater. He became executed then, and sprawled above the worn-out and delighted Jennifer, assisting his weight on his hands and knees. They lay like that during a glad pile, until Darren's cock softened and slipped out of her ass and he rolled to the side.

Jennifer decided to face him, a grin on her face. "That was the best, Darren. You were right; I got here like crazy."

"I'm glad, because it was surely extraordinary for me."

They might have stated extra and executed more, but Stephanie was due home soon, and neither desired her to understand what they were doing. They discussed getting collectively in the future, however those times might have to be arranged. When Jennifer desired a repeat performance, she could name him, and he would make time for her to skip classes and visit her.